The light bulb overhead flickered then came back on, humming like a sick bee. She could hear water dripping somewhere. Plip, plip, plip. There was a skittering sound. Mice, maybe? Maybe not. If she believed in ghosts or monsters, she wouldn't have been caught dead in that laundry room. It was too eerie.

Suddenly, Hilary heard footsteps on the stairs leading down to the basement. She held the basket tightly and ducked down behind the dryer closest to the back wall. As soon as she was crouched down in the cobwebs, she felt stupid. Who was she hiding from? Of course it was some nice woman or man coming down to get their clothes. But if she hopped up now, she'd either scare the person or look even more stupid. So she crouched quietly and listened.

The footsteps came into the room and up to a dryer. The door was opened. There was a second of silence, then the door slammed shut. Another dryer door was opened then slammed. Dust stirred around her head. Hilary squeezed her nose to hold back a sneeze.

The door of the dryer behind which she hid had its door opened. A boy's voice said, "Finally." There was the sound of something being pulled from the dryer. The door slammed shut. Hilary leaned over a little so she could try to see who it was. All she could see was a long shadow on the floor.

Wonderstruck Books is an imprint of Crossroad Press.

Cover illustration by David Dodd
Design by Aaron Rosenberg
ISBN 978-1-941408-63-6

First Crossorad Press Edition

ILLINOIS

THE CEMETERY CLUB

BY ELIZABETH MASSIE

Wonderstruck Books

Many states have legends about ghosts. People claim to have seen ghosts in old houses and hotels, along roadsides, in forests, and in cemeteries. Justice, Illinois, boasts a legend of a ghost in a white dress and black dancing shoes who appears in and around Resurrection Cemetery. She has been nicknamed "Resurrection Mary." Of course, most folks dismiss ghost stories as silly tales of imagination.

But what if a ghost was actually real? And what if that ghost decided to make some serious trouble?

Chapter 1

Frank Simmons stood beside the rumbling washing machine, holding the sheet over his head as his friend, Todd Mickens, cut out two ragged eyeholes. "Hey, be careful," Frank said. "Don't poke my eyes out."

"I will if you keep moving around," said Todd. "Now just hold *still*!"

"We should have just drawn circles where my eyes were first and then—"

"I said hold *still*! I'm almost done. Well, halfway."

The scissors snipped, in and out of the material while thirteen-year-old Frank held as still as he could. Todd, Frank's best friend, was using a little pair of fingernail scissors instead of regular scissors, and it was taking longer than it should have. He worked the scissors around, making two little openings so Frank could see, then stepped back.

"Is that okay?"

"I guess."

"I mean can you see?"

"Yeah, I can see okay."

"Good."

"Does it look stupid?"

"Kind of stupid," said Todd.

"Think it'll scare anyone?"

"I don't know. You need to get some glow-in-the-dark paint. That might make it spookier."

Frank pulled the sheet from his head, balled it up, and threw it on top of the washing machine. His brown hair stuck up on his head, full of static electricity, like the fur of an angry cat.

He and Todd were in the basement laundry room of Frank's apartment building. The two sheets they were using belonged to Mrs. Lancaster on the third floor. She had put her laundry in the dryer and gone back upstairs. She would never figure out who had stolen her sheets.

"How much does glow-in-the-dark paint cost?" asked Frank.

"Five bucks, maybe? I don't know. How would I know? It would be worth it, though, if we want to do this right and really scare some little kids. Paint circles around the eye holes, paint jagged streaks all over the face."

Frank hopped up to sit on a washing machine and banged the heels of his shoes against the white enameled front. Todd leaned back against one of the dryers. He was a little shorter than Frank, and his hair was blond. He had freckles up and down his cheeks.

"We need to get Audrey in on this," he said with a sigh. "She always has extra money."

"Yeah, let's call Audrey. She'll help us out."

"We get the paint this afternoon then tonight we can hang out at the playground and freak out those little brats that come to swing!"

Frank grinned then gathered the sheets up under his

arm. “Let’s do it,” he said.

Frank and Todd raced up the steps from the basement to Frank’s apartment, and, when Mrs. Smith was in the bathroom, made a quick call to Audrey Brooks in hopes she would get them some paint.

Chapter 2

"You're never going to make friends just sitting there," said Hilary's older brother, Douglas. "There are tons of kids around here. Some of them are your age, too. Why don't you introduce yourself to them?"

Twelve-year-old Hilary Wilson sat on the bottom step outside the three-story red brick apartment building. Her arms were crossed over her knees; her chin rested on her arms. Her wavy brown hair was pulled back with a blue clip, with several loosened strands hanging in her face, tickling her nose like little spider legs. Every few seconds she swiped at them, but they just fell back down across her nose. "I just don't want to," she said. "So quit talking about it."

Douglas, a seventeen-year-old boy of medium height and light brown hair, shook his head and smiled. "Believe me, I know you miss Shari. You two were best friends. But she's back in Pennsylvania and we're here in Illinois. There isn't much we can do about that, so why don't you look for a new best friend?"

Hilary glanced up at her brother. The sun was shining from behind him, and she had to squint. Behind Douglas, beyond the parking lot of the apartment complex, traffic roared by on wide, busy Archer Road.

"You think it's that easy?" she asked.

"Well, no, I didn't mean it's easy."

Hilary shook her head. "Mom and Dad didn't even ask us if we wanted to move. It's like they don't care what we want. I was going to be president of the SCA at my old school. I was *popular*! Now I'm just a seventh grader nobody knows. Do you know how awful that is?"

"I can guess."

"I don't think so."

"Hilary," said Douglas with a sympathetic smile. "Everybody has changes in their lives. Mom and Dad didn't just decide to do this without a good reason. You know we have to think about Mom, and about what she needs. Her old job didn't give her time off when she really needed it. Even though it looks like she's doing better now, she has to be able to stay home or go into the hospital if she has to."

Hilary looked away from Douglas. He was right. Mom was sick a lot. It made Hilary sad. And though she didn't want to admit it, it also made her angry.

"Mom's cancer appears to be in remission, but we still need to think of her," said Douglas. "And since Uncle Harry wanted to sell his game store and move to Florida, the move was pretty much perfect for us. Dad and Mom bought the store and they can both work there. If Mom gets sick, she won't lose pay for taking off."

"But the hours at Games Galore are going to be long," said Hilary. "That can't be good for Mom."

"We'll have to see, take it a day at a time. It'll be a compromise. I can step in when they need me."

Hilary let out a noisy breath, pulled a handful of grass from beside the step, and blew it out of her hand. "We didn't get to compromise, Douglas," she grumbled. "We didn't get any say at all."

"It'll be okay. Change can be a good thing. We've only been here a little while, Hilary."

"Did you look across the street, Douglas? We live across from a cemetery! Resurrection Cemetery! How creepy is that?"

"Hilary, just cut it out—" Douglas began.

"I don't want to live here! I don't know anybody. And nobody knows me."

Douglas looked over his shoulder to the parking lot, where his new friend Brian sat in his car, the engine running.

"Listen," Douglas said, looking back at Hilary. "You can't have friends unless you make them. Friends don't just fall out of the sky and drop into your lap. Remember one of Mom's favorite sayings, 'To have friends you have to be a friend.'"

Hilary scowled.

"I have to go with Brian now."

"Sure, fine. Go on."

"Why don't you check out the apartment playground," Douglas said. "There are a lot of kids. And they look nice."

Hilary rolled her eyes. "Only *little* kids play in a playground, Douglas."

"Okay, have it your way." Douglas gave Hilary's hair one last ruffle and hurried down the walk to Brian's waiting car. He waved, hopped in, and the two pulled out of the lot onto Archer Road.

"I'm not a little kid anymore, Douglas, in case you didn't notice!" Hilary called out to the car as it disappeared up the street.

A little boy on a rusty blue bike with training wheels rumbled down the sidewalk that ran the length of the apartment building. Behind him came a smiling mother with her hands outstretched. A moment later, a little girl of about six skipped up the sidewalk with a black puppy on a leash. The puppy yipped and yapped, and the girl scooped him up and took him inside the building. She grinned at Hilary, but Hilary didn't smile back.

Hilary bounced the heels of her shoes on the walk. "They're all little kids around here," she muttered. "Babies! I want to go back to Pennsylvania."

"Hilary!" The voice was her mother's, coming from an open window in their apartment on the third floor. Hilary looked over her shoulder.

"What, Mom?"

"Are you busy?"

Hilary knew if she wasn't busy, her mother would have a chore for her to do. But she wasn't going to lie. She wasn't busy at all, and maybe it would be better doing a chore of some sort than just sitting on the step like a slug.

"Not really," she called up.

"I need your help, then."

Hilary got up, brushed off her jeans, and then went inside through the glass doors. The foyer was narrow but clean. To the right, inside the door, was the row of metal mailboxes. Across from the mailbox was the apartment of the building manager, Mrs. Smith. The Smiths had a son who was in some of Hilary's seventh grade classes, but she rarely saw him around the apartments. There were three other apartments on the first floor, but Hilary didn't know any of the people. She and her family had only lived in Justice for a week, and Hilary had felt shy most of the time.

Hilary climbed the steps to the second floor, then to the third. At the top of the steps was the door to Apartment 9. This was her home. A home that didn't feel like home. She turned the doorknob and walked in.

The living room was small and cheery. The carpet was light blue and the walls white. The furniture, a sofa, loveseat, and recliner, were from the Wilsons' home in Pennsylvania. The family's television had broken during the move, and for now, the television stand stood, empty, in the corner by the window. Mr. Wilson had promised that this weekend he would get a new set.

Hilary's mother was in the kitchen, rattling dishes. Hilary walked through the living room to the kitchen.

"Hey," Hilary said.

Hilary's mother put down the plate she was holding. "Hey, there," she said with a wink. "You look happy."

Hilary shrugged. She tried to smile but couldn't.

"Bored?"

"Maybe." She looked at her mother and frowned. "Doesn't the dishwasher work?"

"Yes. I just prefer to wash them myself. Saves energy and I think I do a better job than a machine."

"Yeah. Whatever."

Mrs. Wilson put her hands on her daughter's shoulders. "Honey, I know how it is to be in a new place. We moved a lot when I was young, and it takes time to adjust.

It even takes time to adjust when you're old, like me."

"You aren't *that* old," she said.

Her mother, a pretty woman with short auburn hair, reached over and gave Hilary a quick hug. "Thanks, Hon. That would raise your allowance if we could afford it. Now, I was hoping you'd do a load of sheets and towels."

Hilary hated doing laundry, but she said, "Okay." Her mother got tired easily, so everyone in the family had to help do as much as they could. They certainly couldn't afford to hire a maid.

As she was digging through the cardboard box of towels and sheets on the floor in her parents' bedroom and sorting some into the plastic laundry basket, her mother called, "Hilary, I've found a lady to stay with you after school and on Saturday mornings. She's young, but she has references for babysitting for the last couple of years. I think we'll give her a try."

Hilary stood straight, her mouth hanging open. "Babysitting!" she snorted. "Wait! Are you *serious*?"

"I'm sorry, Hilary. Poor choice of words. She has good references for being a companion. We don't know anyone here well enough yet and I don't feel comfortable with you having hours alone without me, Dad, or Douglas around. And this will only be for a month or so."

"A *month*? Mom, I'm *twelve*!"

"I know you're twelve."

"Nobody, and I mean *nobody* I know has someone watch them when they're twelve! In fact, some twelve-year-olds babysit little kids themselves!"

"Hilary…"

"I don't need anybody watching me! Please don't hire

her!"

"She's not going to sit and stare at you, Hilary. She's just going to be here in case there is an emergency or something like that. Like if the place catches fire or you fall down and hit your head, or..."

"Mom!"

"And we know how the dark bothers you, when you're alone. It'll be getting dark earlier and earlier."

Hilary cringed. Her mother was right about that. Ever since her mother had been diagnosed, Hilary had found that being alone at night, in the dark, was unsettling. Even scary. It was stupid. At her age, it shouldn't spook her, but it did. Still...

"Mom, don't say that! I don't need anybody to stay with me!"

"Maybe you'll like her, Hilary."

"Just get me a cell phone! If there was an emergency I could call or text you! Everybody in seventh grade has a cell phone!"

"Not everybody..."

"Oh, yeah, they do!"

"Honey, I've told you. Your father and I don't think someone your age needs a phone. Besides, we have a landline here in the apartment."

"Douglas has a cell!"

"He's older. When you're older, we'll reconsider."

"Mom!"

"It's settled, Hilary."

Hilary stood still, looking at the ceiling. She knew her mother had wanted to find someone, but she had hoped she wouldn't be able to. That way, Hilary could prove that staying alone while her parents were at the store and Douglas was doing his high school sports was no big deal. Of course she could handle any emergency that came along without a companion. Without a *babysitter*!

"Did you hear me, Hilary?"

"Yeah," Hilary muttered.

"She'll be here Monday afternoon. Her name is Doreen."

Hilary picked up the basket and carried it past the kitchen to the living room. "You going down now?" asked her mother.

Hilary nodded. She was too mad to talk.

"You need quarters for the machines."

Hilary nodded again. She took the basket to the sofa, dropped it on a cushion, and then went to the kitchen where her mother was holding out a handful of coins. Before Hilary could take them, her mother said, "Hilary, this is a new place. We are all trying to find our way around, trying to find how we fit in, to feel comfortable and make this our home. We're doing the best we can to figure it all out. Please be patient."

Hilary made herself nod.

"We love you."

Hilary nodded again. She took the money and put in into her jeans pocket. She went to the living room, picked up the laundry basket and the small box of detergent that was by the door, and went down to the laundry room in the basement.

Chapter 3

"Put more paint here. It'll make it creepier."

In the bathroom of Frank's apartment, Frank, Audrey, and Todd put the finishing touches of glow-in-the-dark paint on the second ghost sheet. Frank sat on the edge of the tub, his bare feet inside on the pink butterfly no-slip appliques, his jeans legs rolled up to his knees, holding the sheets out while Audrey ran the paintbrush around the eye holes. Todd sat on the closed toilet lid and nodded in appreciation.

"Good idea to do the painting in the tub," Todd said. "We can wash up really good and no one will know we were even here!"

"I'm brilliant," said Frank. "Always remember that."

"Remember what?" asked Todd.

Frank let out an exasperated breath.

Audrey chuckled.

"This is good paint," said Frank. "It dries quick. These will be ready for tonight. I can't wait!"

"You got paint in your hair, Audrey," said Todd.

"Ugh," she said. "Frank, hold the paintbrush."

Frank took the brush and Audrey stood and looked in the mirror over the sink. She had short black hair and cocoa-colored skin. At eleven she was younger than most kids in her class because she'd skipped third grade. She and Frank and Todd had become good friends in sixth grade last year when they had been put on the same social studies project team. They found out that they all liked scary things like zombies, vampires, ghosts, and werewolves, and had gotten an A-plus on the play they'd written and performed, called, "The Terrifying Night at Valley Forge." The play, based on the real events in George Washington's life, was full of ghosts and monsters that came to him in nightmares. The teacher thought it was very creative, even if she wrinkled her nose and cringed during the performance. Audrey, Frank, and Todd were just glad when it was over so they could sit back and make fun of the other sixth graders' dumb projects.

Audrey pulled a drying piece of purple paint from her hair and washed it down the sink. "I hope this doesn't clog the pipes," she said.

"It better not," said Frank. "Now let's get this finished. Mom won't be gone a whole lot longer."

Audrey went back to the tub, dipped her paintbrush into the jar of paint on the tile floor, and made a long, zigzag streak above the eyeholes. "There, that's it for this sheet."

Frank stood up, holding the sheet so it wouldn't fold back on itself and smear, then took the sheet to the bedroom where the first one was laid out across his bed to dry. Frank, Todd, and Audrey looked at their creations.

"Halloween's two weeks away," said Frank. "So the little kids around here won't be expecting this. We'll make 'em jump so high it'll take a year for them to come down again. I love to scare people, don't you? I always have. Even when I was a dumb little kid in pre-school, I would pretend I was a mummy just to watch the teachers scream!"

Audrey crossed her arms, and then said, "Hey, wait, something's wrong here."

"What?" asked Todd.

"We only painted two sheets, if you didn't notice."

"Yeah…so?" asked Frank.

Audrey raised her hands in exasperation. "Hel-*lo*, Mr. Not-So-Brilliant! We learned to count in kindergarten, in case you don't remember. Two sheets aren't enough for three people."

"We weren't counting you."

Audrey's mouth dropped open. "Wait. What do you mean, you weren't counting me?"

"Well, um," said Todd. "You explain, Frank."

Frank crossed his arms and pulled his feet out of the tub. "We were only thinking me and Todd would go spooking kids. We thought you were probably going to be busy or something tonight. Hey, we're going to pay you back for the paint. We already told you that."

Audrey stomped her foot. "So you asked me to buy the stupid paint but thought I'd be too busy to scare kids?"

"Uh," said Todd. "We didn't think you'd want to."

"Don't think much, do you, Todd?"

"Listen," said Frank. "You want a sheet?"

"Well, yeah. Of course I do!"

Frank sighed. At first he'd thought it would be fun, just him and Todd. But Audrey did pay for the paint, and she liked scary stuff as much as they did. "Okay, okay. Sorry. I'll get you a sheet."

"Your mom won't care?" asked Audrey.

Frank went out the door of his bedroom into the hall, then down to the living room. Audrey and Todd trailed after him. "My mom?" he asked, looking back. "She doesn't know anything about it, 'cause we didn't use our sheets. We got them from the laundry room in the basement."

"From who?" asked Audrey.

"From whoever left sheets in the dryer," said Frank. "Jeez, does it matter? It's not like stealing money or anything. Just stupid pieces of cloth. Todd, go get Audrey a sheet."

Todd's eyes widened. "Why me?"

"Because I told you to. Don't make a big deal." Frank sat down on the flowered sofa. Audrey sat on a stood at the kitchen bar.

Todd shoved his hands into his pockets. "What if I get caught?"

"We didn't get caught this morning. You won't get caught. Go."

"I don't want to."

"Just *go*, Todd," said Frank.

Todd kicked at the rug, muttered, "I better not get caught. If I get caught, I'm blaming you. I'm gonna say you made me do it."

Frank made a face.

Todd went out into the hall and pulled the door shut.

Chapter 4

Hilary shoved the last towel into the washing machine then dipped out a scoop of detergent and sprinkled it on top of the clothes. She closed the machine lid, pushed the timer control to get it started, then turned around, picked up the plastic basket, and set it against her hip. This was a spooky place, down here in the laundry room. The lighting was poor; a single fixture in the ceiling, which had sockets for three bulbs, had only one. The shadows that ran across the uneven floor were long and spindly, like a spider's legs. Old socks, molded, slimy, and forgotten, lay like dead eels on the floor against the wall. A pair of old underwear was snagged on the base of one dryer, never to come off in one piece.

Hating things to be messy, Hilary would have picked up the old, wet socks and underwear, but she hated icky things more than she hated mess. She detested touching things that were cold and slippery. Even when she went fishing back in Pennsylvania, she wouldn't bait her hook. The thought of touching earthworms made her skin crawl. When she got a fish on the end of her line, she made Douglas take it off. Fish were quite slimy and wet, too.

So, Hilary thought as she stood in the middle of the

laundry room. *Am I supposed to wait down here until it's finished or can I go upstairs and wait in the apartment?*

She'd done lots of loads of laundry back at her home in Pennsylvania, but this was the first time she'd done laundry here, in a mutual place where lots of people did their wash. Was there some kind of apartment complex laundry rule she was supposed to follow?

The light bulb overhead flickered then came back on, humming like a sick bee. She could hear water dripping somewhere. *Plip, plip, plip.* There was a skittering sound. Mice, maybe? Maybe not. If she believed in ghosts or monsters, she wouldn't have been caught dead in that laundry room. It was too eerie.

Suddenly, Hilary heard footsteps on the stairs leading down to the basement. She held the basket tightly and ducked down behind the dryer closest to the back wall. As soon as she was crouched down in the cobwebs, she felt stupid. Who was she hiding from? Of course it was some nice woman or man coming down to get their clothes. But if she hopped up now, she'd either scare the person or look even more stupid. So she crouched quietly and listened.

The footsteps came into the room and up to a dryer. The door was opened. There was a second of silence, then the door slammed shut. Another dryer door was opened then slammed. Dust stirred around her head. Hilary squeezed her nose to hold back a sneeze.

The dryer door she was hiding behind had its door opened. A boy's voice said, "Finally." There was the sound of something being pulled from the dryer. The door slammed shut. Hilary leaned over a little so she could try to see who it was. All she could see was a long shadow on the floor.

Then the boy's voice said, "Hey, no way, this one has flowers. Flowers won't work!" The dryer door opened, there was the hissing of cloth being shoved back in, and the door slammed shut. Hilary leaned out a little farther, putting her hand down on the tacky, wet floor and grimacing.

The boy was not very tall, with light skin, blond hair, and freckles. He was holding a sheet and staring at it.

"Yeah, okay, here we go," the boy said to the sheet. He balled it up and stuck it under his arm. "This one'll work. Whoever put it in the dryer won't miss it. What's one dumb sheet? Ha!" With that, he disappeared from view. Hilary heard him walk out of the laundry room, into the stairwell, and then up the steps. She stood up and wiped her clammy hand on her jeans.

The boy was stealing sheets.

And she knew him. He was in her English class at school.

Even though Hilary was new to the school, she remembered him. She felt uneasy, knowing he'd stolen something, even if it was only a sheet. Somebody owned that sheet. Somebody paid for that sheet. If someone stole sheets from Hilary's family, it would be hard to replace them. They were watching every penny these days.

Mrs. Smith lived on the first floor, right above the laundry room. As the apartment manager, she should know what the boy had done. Hilary knew she had to tell. She would make it quick, though, because if she was gone very long, her own linens might be stolen.

Dropping the plastic basket to the floor, Hilary hurried out of the room and up the stairs. She paused in the hall in front of Mrs. Smith's door. Should she tell who did it, or just let Mrs. Smith know things were being stolen? She hoped she would know by the time she saw Mrs. Smith face to face.

Hilary knocked on the door. There was movement inside the apartment, and what sounded like giggling.

Hilary knocked again.

The door was bumped from the other side, and the knob turned. It jerked open as far as the chain inside would let it. A boy with dark hair pressed his nose to the crack.

"What do you want?" he asked.

This was Mrs. Smith's son, Frank. "Is your mom home?" Hilary asked.

The boy shook his head, smiling like he knew a joke he wasn't telling Hilary.

"Nope," he said. "Gone shopping. Why?"

"Oh. Well, I just wanted to…" Hilary began. She hesitated, wondering if she could just leave the message with Frank and hope he would tell her. But then, Hilary stopped and stepped back one step.

"Well, what?" asked Mrs. Smith's son. "What do you want?"

"Nothing. Never mind," Hilary said. "Forget it."

"You sure?" grinned Frank.

"I'm…I'm sure," said Hilary.

Another boy's face had come up beside Frank's. It was smiling just as broadly as Frank's. But this boy had light hair and freckles. This boy was the one Hilary saw steal the sheet in the laundry room.

"Okay, then," said Frank. He slammed the door in her face. Hilary could hear the laughing again behind the wood.

Wonderful, she thought in disgust.

Quickly, she went upstairs to tell her mother she would have to sit with the linens until they were done so no one would run off with them. Another wonderful thing about moving to Illinois from Pennsylvania.

Laundry thieves.

Chapter 5

It was six fifteen Saturday evening and almost dark. Todd, Audrey, and Frank stood in the deep shadows around one side of the apartment building complex, flat against the brick wall, peering out at the playground. The three were dressed in their painted sheets. Todd had gotten the giggles and Frank's face was growing hot with anger. If Todd laughed too loudly and gave them away, he'd kick him. They'd worked too hard on this prank to mess it up because Todd couldn't keep his mouth shut. Frank's sheet tickled his face. The eyeholes were lopsided, but he could see pretty well through them.

"Shhh!" he hissed. "They'll hear you."

Todd sniffed, trying to stop giggling. "Okay."

Audrey was quiet, ready.

Most of the little kids had already left the playground with their moms or dads or babysitters, in for Saturday supper. One little boy, however, was still clinging to the swing, begging his mother not to take him inside. The mother was clearly tired, and she was losing her patience.

"Petey," she said as Petey gripped the chains of the swing tightly. "I don't have time to argue with you. Now let go of that swing and come on with me."

Petey, a boy of about six, grinned and shook his head. "Nope!" he said.

Petey's mother put her hands on her hips. "You don't come with me now, I'm going in without you."

Petey leaned back in the swing and looked up at the darkening sky. Then he sat straight and looked at his mother. "Nope!" he said.

Petey's mother said, "We're having hamburgers. You love hamburgers."

"Nope!"

"I mean it!" The mother reached for Petey, but he pushed himself backward in the swing on his tiptoes.

"Nope!"

"I'm going in, then! You'll go to bed hungry."

Petey grinned at her.

"What a brat," whispered Audrey. "His mom ought to just drag him off that swing."

"Shh," said Todd.

"You want to go to bed hungry?" his mother asked.

Petey leaned back in the swing and kicked both feet high up in the air. He swooped forward with the swing, and the mother stepped back.

"All right, then," said his mother. She turned and stalked across the playground gravel to the sidewalk. She looked back once, but Petey wasn't budging. Then she continued walking to the second apartment building and went inside.

It didn't take Petey long to realize he'd been left behind. He suddenly sat straight in the swing, and said, "Mom?"

Mom didn't answer. Mom was inside. "Mom!" Petey

called.

No answer from Mom. Petey stood up from the swing, looking in the direction his mother went. The swing flopped back and forth, knocking Petey in the back of his knees, then going hung still.

"Mom! Come back here!" Petey demanded.

"This is perfect," Todd said under his breath.

Frank whispered, "Ready?"

Audrey and Todd whispered back, "Yeah!"

Petey left the swing set for the sidewalk. "Mom!" he called, sounding both nervous and angry.

"Now!" said Frank.

The three sheet-covered ghosts ran around the corner of the building, heading straight for Petey.

"WHOOOOO ARE YOOOOOOOOU?" Frank wailed.

"WE'RE THE GHOSTS OF THE PLAYGROUND! WE'LL GET YOOOOOOOOOOU!" cried Todd.

Petey's mouth dropped open, but nothing but a little croak came out. He stumbled backward, his eyes wide.

"YOOOOOOOOU SHOULDN'T BE OUT ALONE AT NIGHT!" shrieked Audrey.

"SHAME ON YOOOOOOOOOOOU!" shouted Frank.

Petey began to shake. His lips moved as if he wanted to scream but was too scared to. He looked like a fish out of water.

"YOU BETTER GO HOME TO YOUR MAMA!" cried Audrey.

Audrey, Frank, and Todd, now very close to the boy, raised their arms and flapped the sheets wildly. Squealing, Petey turned on his heels and ran down the sidewalk. He took the steps leading to his apartment building two at a time and disappeared through the door.

The three ghosts stood for a moment. Then Frank broke into loud, uncontrollable laughter. Todd began to laugh, too, and then Audrey. They bent over and laughed until it hurt.

"That was great!" Frank said when he could catch his breath. "Did you see that little kid run?"

"He could win a race he ran so fast!" said Todd.

"The glow-in-the-dark paint really made us extra scary," said Audrey. "I wish I could have had a picture of Petey's face! I thought his eyes were going to pop out of his skull!"

Frank pulled off his sheet. Audrey and Todd did the same.

"Kids like that deserve to be scared," said Frank,

"We better get out of here before Petey's mom comes looking for ghosts," said Audrey.

They trotted back around the corner of the building and balled up the sheets. Frank put them into a plastic garbage bag he'd left on the ground.

"That was fun!" said Audrey. "But I gotta get home."

"Me, too," said Todd.

"Yeah, okay," said Frank. "But we got to come up with something even scarier for next weekend. And then for Halloween, something even scarier than that! Got any ideas?"

"No," said Audrey as she smoothed her hair down and waved. "We'll talk about it at school. We'll figure something out!" She hurried off into the darkness.

"How about you, Todd?" asked Frank. "What can we

do next weekend and Halloween? It's got to be really good, really fun, and really scary!"

"I don't know," said Todd. "I'll talk to you tomorrow, okay?" With that, Todd dashed off into the night, leaving Frank alone with the bag of sheets at his feet.

"Well," Frank said to himself as he picked up the plastic bag and slung it over his shoulder. "We'll come up with something to scare somebody, that's for sure. Scaring people is more fun than anything else!"

Frank, still laughing to himself over Petey's wide eyes and fish-smacking lips, walked home to his own apartment to see what his family was having for supper.

Chapter 6

On Monday morning, Hilary was late to English class. Her locker door had gotten jammed on the cover of her math book, and so she had to find a teacher who then had to find the assistant principal (*So embarrassing!* she thought) who then had to find the master key to open the jammed locker door.

Ugh, she thought as she took the tardy-note and went to class. *What a way to make an impression my second week of school. I'm ten minutes late and everybody is going to stare at me!*

Hilary didn't look at the other students when she entered her English classroom. She handed the note to Ms. Bruce, who was sitting in a student desk in the back of the room. Ms. Bruce read it quickly, and then nodded at Hilary without saying anything. Hilary slipped over to her desk and sat. She put her backpack and cloth lunch bag on the floor. When she finally let herself look up and around, she saw that the class was in the middle of report presentations. Two students were at the front of the room, setting posters up, bumping around behind the podium, and getting ready to talk. The other kids had their evaluation sheets in front of them, pencils poised.

"You're late," said the girl who sat in the row next to Hilary.

"Yeah," said Hilary.

"Get lost?"

"*No.*" Hilary's jaw tightened.

"What happened?"

Hilary looked at the girl. She didn't know the girl's name, but she didn't seem to be making fun and so Hilary said, "My locker got jammed. Stupid math book got caught."

The girl smirked and said, "Yeah, back in sixth grade mine got jammed all the time. This school needs to spend some money and get new lockers."

Hilary smiled a little.

"Get out your evaluation sheet," said the girl as she glanced back at the teacher. "We're getting graded on our comments about other people's reports as well as grades on our own reports."

"Yeah, I know," said Hilary.

"Not too fun," said the girl.

"Not too much," said Hilary. She wondered if this girl might become her friend. She seemed nice enough. Having no friends at all was awful. Hilary felt like a stranger in a country where she didn't even speak the same language.

Hilary dug through her backpack, past her Walter L. Newberry Middle School student handbook and her spiral notebooks, until she found the sheet. She put it on her desk then looked up at the front of the room at the grinning boys who, according to their display, were getting ready to do a report on World War II.

Hilary rated the World War II report pretty highly,

because along with some music from the 1940s, the boys had hand-drawn maps and some old artifacts to show—a helmet, a soldier's journal, lots of black-and-white photos of tanks and trucks. The report that followed, a history of beauty pageants presented by two girls who couldn't seem to stop giggling and hold still, was rated low on both content and presentation. It might have been interesting but the girls just talked about the pageants they'd been in and all the ribbons they'd won. They had a short PowerPoint presentation, but it was just a bunch of pictures of them getting their hair done and posing in their $1,500 dresses. Hilary was glad that she wasn't going to have to do a report. At least that was one good thing about coming to a new school in the middle of the grading period.

Ms. Bruce thanked the pageant girls for their report. As they sat down, she said, "There are eight minutes left before class is over. Do I have any volunteers to go now and get it over with?"

Students shifted in their seats. Hilary looked around, wondering if hands would go up. One did. It was Frank Smith's.

"We'll go," Frank said with a smirk. "We got a really great report, don't we, Todd?"

In the desk behind him, Todd frowned, and then punched Frank in the back. It was clear Todd wanted to wait until tomorrow, but Frank was already standing up and collecting his papers, posters, and a laptop computer. Grumbling, Todd stood up and followed Frank to the front of the room.

What's his report? Hilary wondered. *The fine art of stealing sheets?*

As Frank turned to face the class, he said, "Audrey, you coming or what?"

The girl who had been talking with Hilary groaned, then pulled herself out of her desk and walked up to stand with the two boys.

Oh, that's just great. I guess I can forget about her being my friend if she's friends with those two, thought Hilary sadly.

Frank put the paper report on the podium, hooked his computer to the projector, and spooky music began to wail and whine. On the white board, images of tombstones and mausoleums began to appear in rhythm to the music. Frank motioned to Audrey to hold up a yellow piece of poster board. Drawn on the board, in bold marker lines, was a ghost. The eyes were colored in with red.

What in the world are they going to talk about? Hilary wondered.

"We did a report called 'Haunted Chicago,'" said Frank. He gripped the edges of the podium, leaned forward, and grinned at the class like a cocky salesman. "Me, Todd, and Audrey..."

"Audrey, Todd, and I," corrected Ms. Bruce from the back of the room.

Frank's smile faltered a little but then came back full force. "Audrey, Todd, and *I* researched haunted houses and other places around Chicago. Did you know there was a devil baby in Hull House in 1913? A baby with horns and a tail and feet like a goat? Isn't that the coolest? Well, some people say it was a legend, but we'll let you decide for yourselves!"

Hilary crossed her arms and slid down a little in her

seat. Devil babies? Really? Hilary looked at her evaluation sheet. She wished there was a place to write "really stupid idea."

After a Frank talked a little about the mysterious, devil-like baby that was taken to Jane Addams' settlement house more than 100 years ago, Todd took his place at the podium and told about a Chicago firefighter who died when a building collapsed in 1924.

"His ghostly handprint," Todd said in a low, ominous voice, "was made on the glass at the fire station. It couldn't even be removed with the strongest cleaning chemicals!"

"Ooooh," whispered Audrey from beside Todd, her face scrunched up and trying to sound scary.

"Ooooh," repeated some of the other kids in the classroom, while several others laughed.

Hilary put her elbows on her desk and her head in her hands. On the wall over the chalkboard, Hilary could see that there were only three minutes left in class. Her stomach growled, loudly enough for the boy in the row next to her to look around for the sound. Hilary put her fist against her stomach, hoping it wouldn't happen again.

"And then," said Audrey, who had moved up to the podium for her part in the talk. She narrowed her eyes and talked slowly and softly, like she was trying to scare a bunch of kids around a campfire, "there is Resurrection Mary. She is a ghost that a lot of people around here have heard about. She was killed by a hit-and-run driver way back in 1934. She was on her way home from a dance. A sad, sad story with a scary, scary ending! Mary's been appearing in and around Resurrection Cemetery since 1939."

"Ooooh," whispered Frank with raised eyebrows and widened eyes. He was clearly loving the chance to perform.

"Ooooh," repeated some of the kids, grinning and snickering.

Resurrection Cemetery was the one right across the street from her apartment building. Hilary shook her head and made a face, but the kids up front didn't see it.

"Mary still wears the dress she had worn to the dance," Audrey continued, "and people who have touched her say her skin is very cold."

Hilary looked down at the floor where her cloth lunch bag sat. There was a good lunch inside—a peanut butter sandwich, apple, graham crackers, raisins. Maybe she could just have a couple raisins so her stomach wouldn't growl again. She carefully reached down and pulled open the tab on the bag.

"Once," Audrey was saying, "a man offered Mary a ride in his car. She got in and talked to him in her soft, spooky voice. He looked out at the road, then back at the passenger seat, and Mary had vanished! She didn't even open the door, she just disappeared from the seat!"

Oh, sure, thought Hilary. *Cold-skinned ghosts vanishing through car doors. Audrey can't really believe that crazy stuff.* Carefully, Hilary pulled the small plastic container of raisins out of the bag and into her lap. She lifted the lid.

"At another time, Resurrection Mary bent the metal bars on the cemetery gate," said Audrey. "A policeman saw this and it made the hair on his head stand up straight! He told the cemetery security guard, and they fixed the bars so no one else would wonder what happened and be scared."

Police don't believe in ghosts, Hilary thought dismissively. She slipped a handful of raisins out of the container and into her mouth.

And one went down the wrong way.

Hilary coughed, loudly, sending the container of raisins flying from her lap. Raisins sprayed the air like flies without wings, landing all over the floor and on the shoes of those who sat in desks near her.

"Hey!" laughed the boy in the desk next to hers. "I think Resurrection Mary's in here, throwing raisins around the room!"

Hilary coughed several more times, and the stuck raisin came loose. She swallowed it, then looked back at the boy who had spoken. "Sorry," she managed in a raspy voice.

"Hilary Wilson," said Ms. Bruce from her desk in the back. "What's going on?"

Audrey, Todd, and Frank were standing still at the podium. All were staring at Hilary. Frank was frowning, clearly irritated the report had been interrupted.

"I spilled—" Hilary began. She couldn't believe this had happened. How embarrassing!

"You what?" asked Ms. Bruce.

Hilary swallowed. Her throat hurt where the raisin had been stuck. "I spilled my raisins."

Ms. Bruce clicked her tongue disapprovingly. "Hilary, perhaps you were allowed to eat in class when you lived back in…" She stopped. "Where did you use to live?"

"Pennsylvania."

"Yes," said Ms. Bruce. "Maybe eating in class was allowed in Pennsylvania, but not here. No food. No gum.

No drinks except for bottled water. Please remember that rule. It's in your handbook. Do you understand?"

Hilary nodded. She looked down at the raisins strewn across the floor. She wished the raisins would just disappear, like Mary's ghost did through that car door. She wished she would just disappear, too.

Suddenly, the bell rang. Students were up and out the door in a matter of seconds. Hilary just sat at her desk, waiting, hoping the others would be halfway down the hallway before she left. She knew she had made Frank mad; he hadn't been able to finish his report because of her.

"Will you please clean up that mess before you go to lunch?" Ms. Bruce said finally, standing from her seat.

Hilary nodded.

"Thank you," Ms. Bruce said. Then she smiled. "And don't worry. We all have accidents at some time or other."

Hilary nodded again. Ms. Bruce walked up to her teacher's desk and sat to look at some papers.

A minute later, the raisins were up and dumped into the trashcan. Holding the lunch bag in one hand, Hilary slipped her backpack onto her shoulder and swung through the classroom door into the hallway.

Frank, Audrey, and Todd stood by the wall, waiting for her. Frank put up his hand and said, "Wait a minute."

"What?" Hilary asked.

Frank came up close to her, too close. She backed up a step, then wish she had been brave enough to stand still. Frank was grinning, but his eyes were angry. "You were laughing at us in there," he said.

Hilary's mouth came open in surprise. "What? I was not!"

Todd walked to one side of Hilary. Audrey stood still, her arms crossed and her mouth twisted sideways. She looked like she just wanted to go to lunch.

"Yes, you were," said Todd. "We saw you rolling your eyes at us. And then you messed up our report by spilling raisins. You wanted to mess us up, didn't you?"

"Get out of my way," said Hilary.

"Now we have to finish our report tomorrow."

"Get out of my way."

"Say you're sorry," said Frank.

"I'm not sorry because I didn't laugh at you, it was an accident," said Hilary. She moved forward, trying to break through Frank and Todd, but the two boys closed in more, making a wall. "I said move or I'll call Ms. Bruce."

"Come on, guys, I'm hungry," said Audrey. "Let's go."

"Not until she says she's sorry," said Frank.

"You're the sorry ones," said Hilary, finding a courage she didn't think she had, even as her heart pounded hard in her chest. "Sorry...sorry and stupid. You believe in devil babies and ghosts. I'm a lot smarter than that."

Frank took a deep, furious breath. "You aren't so smart, you think there aren't ghosts." He leaned in close, his nose almost touching Hilary's. "I bet you aren't as brave as you pretend to be. You live in the same building as me. I see you hanging around. You always look scared of something."

"I...I do not!" Hilary shouted. The blood in her arms rushed cold with anger. It felt like bugs were crawling up her throat, and she wanted to scream at this boy and shove him away, hard. But the last thing she needed was to get in trouble in the halls of Newberry Middle School. She managed, "I'm as brave as any of you. Braver. So what?"

"Then," said Frank. He hesitated, finally moving his face back a little and rubbing his lower lip. "Then join our Cemetery Club. We'll see how brave you really are."

"Our…?" said Todd, turning to look at Frank.

Audrey's eyebrows drew together in a question.

"Our Cemetery Club," said Frank. "Don't you think we should let little Miss…what's your name, anyway?"

Hilary almost didn't want to tell him, but couldn't think of a reason not to. "Hilary," she said.

"Hilary," said Frank. He smiled a little smile. "I think we should invite little Miss Hilary to join our Cemetery Club to see just how brave she is. Don't you two?" He looked at Frank and Audrey. They looked at each other then nodded slowly.

Hilary noticed that the hallway was becoming empty. All the other seventh graders were at lunch now. She pointed her finger at Frank. "Get out of my way, Frank."

"Too scared to join our club?" Frank said. "Hilary too scared to be in our Cemetery Club?"

"No," said Hilary. "I'll join your dumb club. I'm not scared of anything. Now get out of my way!" She pushed through Frank and Todd and strolled off toward the cafeteria. She marched with her head high until she reached a side hall, then slipped around into it and leaned back against the wall. Her breaths came in jagged gasps. Her heart continued to slam against her ribs. She hoped Frank, Todd, and Audrey wouldn't see her when the passed by.

What is a Cemetery Club? she wondered. *And why did I agree to join? That was really stupid, Hilary!*

"Excuse me," said a teacher who had come out of her

classroom to find Hilary by her door. She tilted her head and smiled gently at Hilary. "Are you okay?"

"Yeah."

"Are you sure? You look like you don't feel well."

"I'm okay," said Hilary.

"Are you new here?"

Hilary nodded.

"Seventh grader?"

Hilary nodded.

"You should be at lunch. Do you need me to show you where the cafeteria is?"

"No, thanks. I know where it is."

"Then you'd best hurry and get down there."

Hilary nodded and pushed away from the wall.

"But don't run!" said the teacher. "No running allowed in the halls!"

In the cafeteria, Hilary dropped her backpack and lunch bag at an empty spot on one of the tables. She got in line to get milk, thinking, *Next time I'm bringing a water bottle so I can just sit down and eat.*

Seventh graders were clumped in what was supposed to be a straight line, talking and laughing and waiting to get into the kitchen for their burritos and potatoes. It was easy to see who was popular and who wasn't just by their faces and how they stood. Some looked like they owned the world. Others looked like they thought the world was ready to fall down on their heads. Yet others seemed to be in their own worlds apart from everyone else.

I used to be popular. Now I'm nothing. Hilary lifted her head and tried to look like she owned the world but knew she just looked, well, scared. Which is what Frank had said. She made herself smile, and hoped that helped.

As the line moved toward the kitchen door, Hilary again wondered what the Cemetery Club was. Maybe it was nothing. Maybe it was just a made-up thing that Frank wanted to challenge her with. Well, she wouldn't bring it up again unless Audrey, Todd, and Frank did. And no matter what, she'd be as tough as they were. She wished her friend Shari was here. They would have laughed out loud at the three kids and their report.

Ghosts, Hilary thought. *Ridiculous!*

Chapter 7

"What in the world is a cemetery club?" Audrey asked after Hilary had hurried off down the hall toward the cafeteria.

Frank, Audrey, and Todd were on their way to lunch, walking slowly. They liked to get to the cafeteria late because the line was always shorter. Of course, there were a couple times they'd been caught in the hall by the teachers and had gotten fussed at, but that didn't keep them from trying.

"It's a club," said Frank, tilting his head back and feeling pretty good about himself. "A club I just made up in my head."

"Okay, yeah, I figured that. But what is it?"

"I don't know yet, exactly. But that girl Hilary was laughing us. She thought we were stupid. She thinks she's so brave. We're going to prove to her that she's not."

Todd made a face. "You made it sound like the three of us really believe in ghosts and stuff like that. We don't."

"I know that. And you know that. But I think we can scare her better if she thinks we do. We can play it up real good!"

"Hey," said Todd, pausing to dig in his jeans pocket.

"Can I have some lunch money?"

"No," said Frank. "You never pay me back."

"Audrey?" Todd asked. "Can I borrow lunch money?"

"You never pay me back," Audrey said. "Why don't you ever remember to bring money? Why don't you just pay for the whole month like most people do? Then you wouldn't have to deal with it each day."

"Because half the time I hate what they have for lunch, and so I'd rather spend the money on something else."

Frank frowned. "But if you keep money for when you like the lunch, why do you always end up asking us for money?"

"Um," said Todd, patting his pockets even more furtively, "I have the money. I just don't remember where I put it."

"Good grief, Todd," groaned Audrey.

"So what do you want me to do?" said Todd. "Starve to death?"

Frank and Audrey didn't reply.

They reached the door to the cafeteria. Frank peeked in to see if any teachers were watching. When none seemed to be looking at the door, he said, "C'mon."

The three hurried in and sat quickly at the nearest table. They put their backpacks on the seats, and then went up to get in line. As usual, the line was very short. Most of the kids had already gone through.

Glancing around, Frank saw Hilary sitting by herself at a table near the stage. It looked as if she didn't like her burrito. She was picking at it and staring ahead.

Frank turned back around and picked up a tray. He didn't know what the Cemetery Club was going to be, but it was going to be fun. Scaring people was such a kick. Tonight, he would figure it out and let Audrey and Todd know.

"Please," said Todd, squishing up his eyes and looking pathetic. "Please let me borrow lunch money. I like burritos. I'll pay you back tomorrow. I promise."

Frank grumbled and pulled several dollars from his pocket. He handed them to Todd, knowing he'd probably never see them again. But at least, Todd owed him. He could pay back in other ways.

"Thanks!" said Todd. He took a milk carton and waved the money at Audrey, who shook her head and said, "Cool it, Todd."

Chapter 8

The key slipped into the lock and the front door popped open. Hilary came into the living room and dropped her backpack on the sofa. She glanced at the empty television stand. Her father had promised they'd get a new TV soon. She hoped so. Not that she loved to sit in front of the tube that much, but there were a couple shows she really liked.

"Anybody home?" she called.

Then she remembered that Mom and Dad were both at Games Galore today, their first full day since moving to Illinois. Today until long after supper. Today and most every day from now on, except Sundays. Which meant…

Oh, no! How could I have forgotten?

"Hello!" came an unfamiliar voice from the bathroom.

Hilary stood in the middle of the living room, waiting, her hands drawn up into fists of frustration. *I should just leave now, pretend I'm not home, and then…*

But then Doreen came down the hall into the living room. She was young, like Hilary's mother had said. She had short blonde hair and glasses. She was smiling.

"Hi there, Hilary. I'm Doreen," the young woman said. "Your mother said you'd get home at three forty-five, so I'll be here each day at three thirty."

Hilary shoved her hands into her pockets.

"How was school?"

"Okay. I'm going to my room. I have homework to do."

Doreen put her hands on her hips and nodded. "All right, sure. But first, I've got chocolate chip cookies baking in the oven. They'll be done in about five minutes. You can have a snack and then do your homework."

"No," said Hilary. She picked up her backpack and brushed around Doreen. Without looking back, she said, "I have to do it now." She went into her bedroom and slammed the door shut. She sat on the edge of her bed and stared at the wall.

There were footsteps outside the door. Doreen said, "Hilary, are you all right?"

"I'm fine," said Hilary. "I have to do my homework."

"The cookies are going to be really good."

"I'm not hungry. I'm just really busy." *You eat the dumb cookies, I don't want them!*

There was a pause. Then Doreen said, "All right."

There was the sound of a sigh and then the feet went away from the door.

Tears sprang into Hilary's eyes. She hated it here. It wasn't fair. Shari was back in Pennsylvania with all of Hilary's other friends. Shari didn't have a babysitter in the afternoons. Shari didn't have three kids threaten her in the hall at school.

"And Shari's mom's not sick so much," she whispered then felt bad she'd said it. She loved her mom. But Mom was supposed to be better. It was just too hard to think about sometimes.

Hilary lay on the bed, pulled her pillow into her chest, and cried. She didn't come out of her room until eight o'clock, when Douglas returned from basketball practice.

Chapter 9

"I thought we were going to keep scaring the little kids," said Todd. His voice was whiny. "That was the plan. Do scarier and scarier things until Halloween."

Frank, Audrey, and Todd sat on the swings at the apartment building's playground. It was Wednesday afternoon. A few little kids were also on the playground, over at the sliding board and seesaw. They kept looking over at the three older kids like they didn't trust them. The mothers sat on the benches and talked with each other. It was cold today; leaves that had dropped from the nearby maple trees raced across the ground in the breeze, chasing each other like dogs after cats. Frank wore his denim jacket. Todd had on his hooded sweatshirt. Audrey was in her red coat.

"That was Saturday. Things have changed," said Frank. He picked a blade of dead grass and ran it through his teeth, then grinned widely with his lips drawn back.

"You look like a redneck," said Todd.

"I look like the brilliant person that I am," said Frank, still grinning. Audrey laughed and twisted herself around in her swing, then let it go, causing her to spin in a dizzying circle with her coattail flying.

"Okay, so here's the thing," Frank said, pulling the grass back out again and tossing it to the ground. "We have to figure out the Cemetery Club. I been thinking and I got some good ideas."

Todd dragged the toes of his shoes back and forth in the dirt dips beneath his swing. "Like what?"

"Hilary thinks she's so cool. She acts so stuck up at school, I'm sure you noticed."

Todd nodded.

"We tell her that to join the club, she has to show how brave she is. Then we scare her until she can't take it anymore. When she finally gives in, we win."

"Win what?"

Frank shook his head and grunted. Todd was so thick sometimes. "We just *win*. We proved we are braver than she is so we *win*."

"Oh. I'd rather have a prize for winning."

Frank ignored this. "I say we figure out something for Friday night," he said. "Something to scare her. The club will meet every evening until Halloween. We probably won't have to meet that long. She'll be really scared long before then and quit."

"And that means we won!" said Todd.

"Yep," said Frank.

"I still think we should get a prize."

Frank groaned.

"So tomorrow at school we tell her the initiation begins Friday night," said Audrey. "That'll make her worry all day what's going to happen."

Todd grabbed the swing chains and swung back and forth for a minute, thinking. Then he said, "You can buy night crawlers at the convenience store down the block."

Frank patted Todd on the shoulder. "Now you're thinking. We can do something with big fat worms!"

Audrey said, "Some people aren't scared of worms."

Todd didn't say anything. He ran his foot back and forth in the dirt.

"What about you, Todd?" asked Audrey. "You scared of worms?"

"No," he said, but his voice didn't sound convincing. "I don't mind worms."

"Ha!" said Frank. "Todd's scared of worms!"

"I am not, now shut up."

"Well," said Audrey, "what if Hilary's not scared of worms? The initiation will be a bust."

"We'll make it so she *is* scared," said Frank. "We're smart, we can come up with a great idea."

"Let's go get some now before it gets dark," said Audrey. "Then I can go on home. My feet are getting cold."

"You got some money?" asked Frank.

"Not this time!" said Audrey. "I always pay for stuff."

"How much do worms cost, Todd?" asked Frank.

"Why would I know?" answered Todd.

"I don't think they cost much, Audrey," said Frank.

"I'm not paying for anything else for a while. This bank is closed!"

Frank turned to Todd. "Go to your apartment and ask your dad for the lunch money you owe us. We'll use that for the worms."

"I can't," said Todd. "He's sleeping."

"Then wake him up."

"He'll be mad."

"Look in his wallet, then," Frank said. "He's got to have some money in his wallet."

"Are you kidding? No way, Frank," said Todd. "Forget the worms."

Frank hopped off his swing. He scowled and stamped his feet on the ground. One of his shoes had a hole in the toe, and his feet were cold. "I'm going in. See you guys at school." He stalked off, leaving Todd and Audrey at the swings.

Nothing will stop me from having a really scary Cemetery Club, he thought as he walked. *I'm going to scare that Hilary girl bad!*

He climbed the front steps of his building and pulled open the heavy front door. Inside the foyer he stopped and thought, *If I can't find money in my apartment, I'll go to the convenience store and get the night crawlers, anyway. It won't be the first time I've stolen something and gotten away with it.*

Chapter 10

Hilary tried to get back to her bedroom before Doreen knew she was home on Thursday, but it didn't work. The babysitter, or the *companion*, as her mother was now making a point to call her, had been looking in a kitchen cabinet when Hilary tiptoed into the apartment. She whirled around the moment Hilary tried to sneak past the kitchen door.

"Hi, there!" Doreen said cheerfully.

Hilary sighed. She let her backpack drop to the floor, keeping her fingers wrapped around the strap. "Hey."

"How was school?" Doreen's eyebrows went up as if she was trying to look really interested. Hilary knew she wasn't. Babysitters didn't care. They just pretended to care so they could keep their jobs.

"How much does Mom pay you?" asked Hilary.

"What? Well," said Doreen, "that's between me and your mom."

"I would think it would be more than a cell phone."

"I don't know about that."

"If I had a phone, I wouldn't need a babysitter. Everybody in seventh grade has a phone but me."

“There’s a phone right here in the kitchen. And I’m not here to babysit.”

“You’re here to watch me, just like a babysitter.”

“Honey, please listen.”

“I’m not your honey.”

“I’m sorry. Hilary. Listen, I know I’m not hired to come here forever. This is temporary. I’m sure your parents told you that. And just having a phone doesn’t necessarily make someone safer. I’m sure your parents explained that, too.”

Hilary rolled her eyes.

“She just wants you to be safe until…”

“Until what? Until I’m in high school?” Hilary demanded. “Until I’m, what, twenty? Until I’m old and dead?”

Doreen sighed and gave Hilary a sympathetic smile. “Just until your parents feel safe here in this new place. That may sound strange, but maybe this is more about your mom than about you. You’re not scared of being in a new home, a new city, but your mother might be, and doesn’t want to tell you. Give her time, Hilary.”

Hilary considered this. At least Mom didn’t tell Doreen that Hilary didn’t like darkness.

“In the meanwhile, can we at least get along?” asked Doreen. “I have a feeling I won’t be hired to stay with you for long. Can’t we be friends until then?”

Hilary let out a loud, frustrated breath. “Fine,” she said. “Did Douglas call this afternoon? He said he thought his basketball practice might be cancelled today.”

“No,” said Doreen. “Nobody called but your dad. He said to tell you that the new television should be arriving today before five. He thought that would cheer you up."

"Oh," said Hilary. It was good news, but she wasn't going to let Doreen know she thought it was good news.

"Good, huh?" asked Doreen.

"Whatever." Hilary picked up her backpack and went to her bedroom. When she opened the door, she gasped.

Doreen came up behind her. "What do you think?"

I don't believe it!

"My sister had to borrow my car today and she dropped me off a half hour early. With the extra time, I thought I'd go ahead and get this done. I knew you had other things on your mind what with school and all, and so I decided to help out. I think it looks pretty," said Doreen. "Don't you?"

Hilary's whole room was rearranged. Her bed had been moved from the middle of the room and was now beneath the window. Dolls Hilary hadn't looked at in five years had been taken out of the packing boxes and were now arranged tidily on her pillow. They grinned as if to say, "Hey, Hilary, we're back whether you want us or not!" The horse posters Hilary had laid out on her dresser to put up on her wall were rolled up with rubber bands and propped up against her desk. On the wall where the posters were going to go were two framed flower pictures Hilary's mother had had on the bathroom wall back at the old house in Pennsylvania. Shoes, which had been scattered here and there, were lined up along the baseboard as if they had marched there.

Hilary stepped into her bedroom. She stared.

"If you'd put your backpack on the desk each afternoon," said Doreen. "You could keep your room looking clean. A clean room helps people feel more comfortable and at home."

Opening her closet door slowly, Hilary saw that Doreen had even rearranged her clothes. Her clothes were hanging, color-coded. Reds to purples to blues to greens to oranges. It looked like a clothes rainbow.

"I don't believe it," Hilary whispered.

"I'm glad you like it!" said Doreen.

Hilary spun around, her finger pointing at Doreen. "I *don't* like it!" she shouted. "I hate it! You don't have the right to mess around with my stuff! You shouldn't even be here! I'm too old for a babysitter! I hate this! I hate this place and I hate you!"

Doreen's mouth dropped open, but before she could say anything, Hilary pushed past her.

"Hilary!" cried Doreen. "Where are you going?"

Hilary ran into the living room, scooped her jacket from the loveseat, and yanked the front door open. She didn't even stop to shut the door behind her. Her heart slammed and her head pounded like a train on tracks. She raced down the steps to the first floor. Behind her, back up the steps, she heard Doreen calling for her to come back.

Out of the apartment building she ran, across the parking lot to the curb on Archer Road. Then she stopped, leaned over, and tried to keep from crying. Her throat felt like it was full of sharp pieces of gravel.

The traffic was heavy on the wide highway. It was four o'clock, the beginning of rush hour. People were trying to get home for supper and a relaxed evening with their families.

When a break came in the traffic, Hilary hurried

across to the other side, and then stopped. She slipped on her jacket and zipped it up.

In front of her was Resurrection Cemetery. It was a huge place, one that she'd only seen from her side of the street. As far as she could see in both directions, the iron fence stretched along the sidewalk. She walked to the fence and put her hands out to touch it. Inside, were vast stretches of well-trimmed lawn covered with countless headstones and mausoleums. There were trees and narrow, paved roads leading here and there within the graveyard. Patches of autumn flowers bloomed in yellows, oranges, and reds.

Hilary walked along the sidewalk a few blocks to the large main gate. To each side of the paved gateway were square, concrete pillars. Separating an entrance and exit road was a larger pillar with "Resurrection Cemetery" engraved on it. Hilary wondered how old this cemetery was. It was certainly the biggest one she'd ever seen. She took a deep breath and walked inside.

Of course, she'd been in cemeteries before. Back in Pennsylvania, her father would take the family for Sunday afternoon drives. Sometimes, the drive would take them into one of the local cemeteries. There, Hilary's mother, who was very interested in history, took photos of old and interesting headstones. Hilary, Douglas, and their father would walk around to find people who shared their first names, or people who had lived the longest or who had died at the youngest age. Hilary was fascinated with the beautiful stone angels that some families could afford to put up in honor of their loved ones. Douglas would read aloud the inscriptions on the stones of those who had died in wars. The Wilsons had respect, not fear, of graveyards.

And it wasn't dark yet, so that was good, too.

Hilary followed the main road to the right. At an intersection, Hilary walked left. As she went, she read the last names of the stones closest to the road. Kelly. Jones. Norman. Scott. Some of the stones were little and had lambs on top of them. Hilary guessed those were the graves of children. Sometimes accidents took people away from their families. Sometimes violence. Sometimes old age. And sometimes sickness, like cancer.

Stop thinking like that, she told herself sternly. She turned her attention to the arrangements people had placed in memory of those who had died. Some flowers were plastic, some were fresh. Some were affixed to Styrofoam in the shapes of crosses; some were stuck in baskets.

It seems like a lot of money for nothing, she thought. *The dead person doesn't know about the flowers.* But then she thought, *Well, maybe it makes the families feel better.*

Stepping off the road, Hilary walked across the grass to a large maple tree. The leaves were half-gone from the branches, having fallen to the ground around the trunk and tossed far and wide by breezes. Those that still hung to the branches were brown and crispy. It was a tall tree, with limbs that stretched out like it had just awakened from a good nap. Hilary had had a tree like this in her back yard in Pennsylvania. It had been a good climbing tree.

Looking around to make sure no one was watching, Hilary caught the lower branches in her hands and scrambled up the tree. She sat on a limb for a moment, then stood carefully, glanced above for the next good handhold, then climbed up to another, higher limb. She scooted around to get comfortable, then gazed out at the cemetery from her new perch.

From this vantage point, Hilary could see a lot of the cemetery. She kept one hand on a branch above for balance, then turned to see in all directions. To the north, among the many other headstones, a man and woman stood over a grave, wiping their eyes and staring at the newly placed sod. To the east, Hilary could see a thick grove of evergreen trees, and a small fenced area that must have had some very old graves inside. To the west, down a knoll under a bright blue tarp, a funeral was being held. People stood around, moving very little, dressed in dark clothes. A teen stood apart, texting on his phone as if he had better things to do. Hilary wondered about the family. Who had died? A grandparent? A child? A mother?

She sat silently, watching the people come in and out of the cemetery. Watching as the sun began to lower itself behind the trees and monuments to the west.

"What are you doing up there?"

Hilary flinched and nearly lost her grip on the branch over her head. She looked in the direction of the voice. Down on the ground near the tree, leaning on a large gray stone marker engraved "Patrick Oliver O'Toole," was a girl who looked to be about seventeen. She had long blonde hair pulled back in a ponytail. She wore a thin white dress with a blue shawl around her shoulders. Her shoes were black.

"I'm sitting, if it's all the same to you," said Hilary.

"Oh, gosh, I don't mind," said the girl. "Sorry if startled

you. You can sit up there all day if you want."

Hilary smiled a little. This girl seemed friendly enough.

She must have been with those folks having the funeral, Hilary thought. But she decided not to ask; that would be rude.

"I wish I could climb a tree," said the girl.

"Why can't you?" asked Hilary.

"I don't want to mess up my clothes."

"Oh," said Hilary. "I thought you meant you didn't know how to climb a tree."

The girl laughed lightly and put her hands on her hips. "Of course I know how to climb a tree. Who doesn't? So, you're up there, but why are you up there?"

"Just watching people," said Hilary. "It's fun, spying on people when they don't know you're there."

"Were you spying on me?"

I don't want her to think I was spying on her family having a funeral, if that really is her family.

"I didn't even know you were there," said Hilary. "You must be really quiet."

"What happens if you spy on things you wish later you hadn't seen?" the girl asked.

"I…I don't know," said Hilary. "That's never happened to me. I'm not that good at spying yet. I'm not a professional spy, you know. I'm just a level-one spy. A spy-in-training. When you're a spy-in-training, you have to sit in trees. When you're a real spy, they give you sunglasses, a passport, a long scarf, and a really cool car."

The girl chuckled, then sat down on the grass beside Mr. O'Toole's headstone. She crossed her legs carefully.

She said, "What's your name?"

"Hilary," said Hilary. "What's yours?"

"Marjorie."

"Where do you live?"

"Not too far from here. How about you?"

Hilary freed one hand to point across Archer Road. "In the apartment complex over there. I used to live in Pennsylvania. We just moved two weeks ago."

"Do you like it here?"

"Not so much. I don't have a lot of friends yet."

Marjorie picked up the plastic basket of flowers at the base of Mr. O'Toole's headstone. She held it up for Hilary to see. "What do you think of these flowers? They stay bright for a long time, and they don't lose their petals. But I think they're kind of ugly. They don't smell good."

"You're right. They just smell like plastic."

"They never used to have things like this. Flowers used to always be real."

Hilary planted her feet on the branch below her and lowered herself down. Then she grabbed a wobbly limb and swung her feet out over the ground. She dropped into the leaves under the tree. She brushed herself off, and then sat down in the leaves a few feet away from Marjorie. Closer now, she could see that the girl's eyes were blue.

"What do you mean, they never used to have things like that?" Hilary said, nodding toward the plastic basket that Marjorie had put back down. "I've always seen plastic flowers in cemeteries."

Marjorie just shrugged and put the flowers back down. She drew her shawl around her shoulders and stared out past Hilary to the funeral, which was now coming to a close. People were beginning to wander away.

"Were you with those people?" Hilary asked, and then suddenly wished she hadn't.

"No, I'm just walking around," Marjorie said. "I like it here. It's quiet. What about you?"

Hilary decided to tell the truth. It couldn't hurt anything. "I'm hiding," she said. "I'm mad at somebody back at my apartment."

"Really?" asked Marjorie. She leaned forward, seeming to be interested in this little bit of gossip. "Who?"

"I don't really want to say." She would not tell somebody she didn't know that she had a babysitter—not only a babysitter, but also an intrusive one who even wanted to tell her how to arrange her bedroom! "But I'm going to stay here until this person really gets worried and wonders where I am. I want her to wonder if I ran away, or got kidnapped, or got hit by a car."

"You're really mad, aren't you?"

"Well, of course I am! And I'm not going back until it's dark. I might not go back until after midnight!" *No, I would never stay out alone that long in the dark, but Marjorie doesn't need to know that!*

"They do lock the cemetery, you know," said Marjorie. "In fact, nobody gets out of here…alive!" Marjorie made a spooky face. Both she and Hilary laughed.

"If that happens," said Hilary, "I'll just find a tree and climb up in it and not let the guards see me."

Suddenly, Hilary heard voices nearby on the road. She looked around the tree and saw an old couple strolling arm in arm along the pavement just several yards away. They were heading toward the main gate, talking and smiling, happy, it seemed, just to be together. Hilary watched them for a moment. It was strange but nice to see really happy people. Hilary realized that for quite a long time now, she hadn't been happy at all. Mainly, it was because of the move. Because she missed Shari and didn't have any other friends. Because her mother was sick.

Hilary turned back around to speak to Marjorie.

But the girl was gone.

Hilary stood and looked around. Marjorie was nowhere to be seen. She'd probably realized it was late and had to hurry home. She must have run off through the tombstones.

"See you later," Hilary said to the cold air of the cemetery, wondering if she really would see Marjorie again.

Hilary then realized that Marjorie was right. They would surely lock the cemetery gates soon. And being locked inside would really suck.

As she walked along the road toward the cemetery entrance, hunched over to keep warm, a strong gust of wind rushed by her. It caught in her hair and tangled it into a thick knot. In the wind, Hilary thought she could hear a voice wailing. It sounded like a lonely voice, a frightened voice, the voice of a ghost. If she didn't know better, she would have been afraid.

But of course, she thought to herself as she glanced over her shoulder to make sure nothing peculiar was behind her in the fading sunlight, *there are no such things as ghosts.*

Chapter 11

The night crawlers were great, slimy, and wiggly once they got warmed up. Frank had them out on his bed, watching them try to burrow up under his bedspread. They left trails of black soil, which Frank had figured out was worm poo, but he didn't care. He had already named all twelve—Stinky, Sticky, Stubby, Slippy, Slinky, Sloppy, Slappy, Snickers, Sneakers, Snappy, Snippy, and Arnold. He wasn't sure which one was which except for Arnold, who had a much lighter band around its middle than the others. Frank still didn't know exactly what he, Todd, and Audrey were going to do with them, but somehow, these stolen worms would make a real good surprise for Hilary Wilson.

I can't wait until tomorrow, he thought. *This will be so much better than scaring little kids!*

A couple worms slowed down and began to twist back and forth against the sheet. Frank noticed they were drying out. He scooped up all twelve, ran them to the bathroom and wet them down under the faucet. Then he put them back into the soil-filled container and hid the container under his bed.

Chapter 12

Hilary stood outside her apartment door. Her parents were home from Games Galore; she had seen their car in the parking lot in front of their apartment building. She told herself she had no idea what they were going to say to her, but she really knew. And it wasn't going to be very pleasant.

"Yeah, but having a babysitter isn't very pleasant, either," she said aloud to herself. Since she hadn't taken a key with her, she knocked on the door.

It was less than five seconds before the door was jerked open, and Hilary was face to face with her father. At first he looked worried. But then his face folded into wrinkles of anger.

"Hilary!" he shouted.

Hilary stood in the hallway, wanting to come inside so the neighbors wouldn't hear, wanting to get it over with.

"I'm sorry, Dad," she said, glancing at the floor.

"Where on Earth have you been?"

"May I please come in first?" Hilary asked.

With a grunt, Mr. Wilson stepped back to let Hilary come into the living room. Standing in the middle of the floor were Douglas and Mrs. Wilson.

“Hilary,” said Mr. Wilson. “I asked you. Where have you been? We’ve been so worried! Doreen called us at the store and said you had run off without a trace.”

“If I had a cell phone you could have called me to find me,” Hilary mumbled, then felt terrible she’d said it.

Hilary’s mom took a sharp breath, but didn’t respond to Hilary’s complaint. Her father continued, “Doreen said you were upset because she’d done some cleaning, and then you told her you hated her and didn’t need a babysitter. I was just sick about the whole thing when I heard! We closed up the store and came home right away. When Douglas got here, we went to nearly every apartment, looking for you. I was getting ready to call the police, did you know that?”

The police? Hilary couldn’t believe they were *that* worried. “No,” she said. “I didn’t know that.”

Mrs. Wilson put her hand to her forehead and sat down on the loveseat. Douglas put his hand on her shoulder.

“So where were you?” Hilary’s father repeated.

“Just across the street for a while,” said Hilary, “and then I went to the laundry room and hung out and watched people wash their clothes.” It was the only place she could find, beside home, where she wouldn’t be alone after dark. There were a couple moms down there, and she’d even helped them sort colors. “Where’s Doreen? She can tell you what made me so angry!”

“We told her she could go home. She felt really bad about this. She said she didn’t know what was the matter with you, but that you just got angry and stormed out. Poor Doreen, she thought it was her fault.”

“But it *was* her fault!” shouted Hilary. “Did you see what she did to my bedroom? She got all in my stuff without permission! She didn't have a right to do that!"

"What are you talking about?" asked Mrs. Wilson.

"She rearranged everything in my bedroom! Didn't she tell you? Didn't you see that?"

"No," said Hilary's father.

"She moved my posters, my bed, and she even took all my clothes down and hung them back in the closet the way *she* thought they should go!"

Mrs. Wilson looked at Mr. Wilson. "I wonder why Doreen did that?"

Mr. Wilson stood silently for a moment, looking from Hilary to Mrs. Wilson. "Oh," he said quietly.

"Oh, what?" asked Hilary's mother.

"I think I see what happened."

"What happened?" asked Hilary's mother.

Mr. Wilson let out a sigh and put his hands into his pocket. "I think this is partly my fault. I asked Doreen if she'd help out with the cleaning for just one day. I told her I'd pay her a little extra if she'd do some of the heavy work, like cleaning Hilary's room. I thought it was a good idea. I thought it'd be a nice surprise."

"Dad!" said Hilary.

"Hilary, your room hasn't been straight since we moved in. Boxes still in the floor, dust and grit and clothes everywhere. I thought it would be easier if you had some help. Maybe Doreen just got a little overly enthusiastic."

"She shouldn't have done what she did!" said Hilary.

"Hilary, I'm sorry. I'll call Doreen and tell her what happened and explain the misunderstanding."

"But," said Mrs. Wilson, looking exhausted and sad, "that's still no reason to scare us so badly."

Hilary stomped her foot. "Listen to me!" she shouted. "I'm too old for a babysitter or a companion! It's not fair that I have to stay with her! How many other twelve-year-old kids have to stay inside their apartments with a baby-sitter? Doreen makes me sick!"

Douglas pushed at the air with his hands. "I'll let you guys figure this out." He walked down the hall toward his bedroom.

"Hilary, sit down," said Mr. Wilson. Hilary sat on the chair beside the television stand. Mr. Wilson sat on the loveseat beside his wife. He looked very tired now, and not so angry. "I know things aren't like they were back in Pennsylvania."

"No kidding," Hilary mumbled.

"Please be quiet, Hilary, and let your father talk," said Mrs. Wilson. Hilary closed her mouth even as words wanted to rush out again.

"Hilary," he said again. "We love you and want the best for you. I'm sorry you don't like Doreen, but she seems fine to us and I think she likes you. We want her to continue doing the job for which we hired her, for a little while longer. Until we feel more comfortable in our new place. Until you're more comfortable being alone at night."

"I'd be okay if you got the TV you promised! I could turn it on and it would be like someone was there!"

"Hilary, stop it."

Hilary slumped down in the chair and stared at her toes.

"However, we'll try to give you a little more freedom. I understand that you don't want to have to stay in the apartment all the time after school. So, what I'll do is this. If you get permission from Doreen, and she knows exactly when you are going to be back, we'll let you go out in the afternoons for a half hour. No more. You're to be back before it gets dark. And you are to stay on the property of the apartment building. You are not to wander off anywhere else."

Hilary let out a long, silent breath.

"For now, it's that or nothing."

Hilary's mouth twitched but she stayed silent.

"Now," said her mother. "That means you check it out with Doreen first. And we mean it. Half an hour. Stay on the property. If you break those rules, you'll go back to the way it was. What do you say?"

"Whatever," said Hilary.

"Is that a yes?"

"Yes."

Mrs. Wilson stood up and walked over to Hilary. She gave her a kiss on top of her head and said, "I've got to go to bed." She went down the hallway. Hilary could hear the bedroom door open, then shut.

Mr. Wilson linked his fingers over his knees. "Hilary," he said quietly, "please try to help us out. Your mother and I are working very hard. We leave the apartment in the morning. We don't get home until long after supper. We're trying to get the game store up and going and profitable, and it's not very easy. Hopefully, when we make enough money with it, we can hire someone else to work for us so one of us can come home earlier. But for now, it's just your mom and me. And even though she doesn't say it, she gets tired so easily. You know she's still not completely well. Even though she had the cancer treatments back in Pennsylvania and even though she hasn't had any real bad times in the past month, we must take care. I want to make things as easy on her as possible. And not having to worry about you would help."

Hilary felt her teeth grind down on each other. Here it came again. The "be good because your mom might be in remission but she's not totally well yet" speech. Hilary felt bad that it made her mad, but she couldn't help it. She loved her mom, so much it hurt sometimes, but it seemed Hilary and Douglas always had to be extra quiet or extra good or extra clean or extra anything, everything, because their mom was sick.

Hilary nodded while her father was talking and said nothing. When he was finished and had kissed her good night, Hilary went into her bedroom and shut the door. A second later, her father tapped on the door.

"Speaking of TV, I just wanted to let you know that television came today," he said. "You see it?"

"No."

"Well, it's here. Still in the cardboard box, though, back against the wall where some of the other boxes are that we haven't gotten to. I'll set it up tonight."

"Sure, okay," Hilary said. "G'night."

Her father walked away from the other side of the door. Hilary stared at the rearranged furniture, her rolled-up posters, and the clothes hanging in the closet. Tears of frustration, sadness, and loneliness sprang into her eyes. "See how you like this when you come tomorrow, Doreen," she said, and then she began to put everything back the way it was in the first place.

Chapter 13

"Doreen," said Hilary. "I'm going to play video games at Frank Smith's apartment." She added, "Would that be okay?"

It better be okay, she thought.

Doreen was watching an afternoon talk show on the family's new television, her feet up on the loveseat armrest. She had a bowl of popcorn on the coffee table. Doreen hadn't seemed upset about Hilary's room being back the way it was. Doreen just didn't seem to get upset about much at all. Except, of course, running off. Doreen's calm drove Hilary crazy.

"Where does he live?" Doreen asked as she turned to look at Hilary.

Hilary stood beside the front door, pulling on her jacket. "Downstairs in apartment number one. His mom's the apartment manager. He's in my English class at school." She hesitated, waiting for Doreen to say something, but Doreen was looking at the television screen again. It was something about exercise or weight loss or nutrition. One of those "get healthy" episodes.

"Doreen," said Hilary. "Is it okay if I go?"

Doreen looked over again. "Oh, yes, of course. A half hour, remember."

"Wait, no. If it's actually in the apartment building, I have an hour."

Doreen looked at Hilary, her head tilted uncertainly. "I don't think so..."

"Yeah, that's the rule. Half hour outside, hour if I say in the building. Don't worry. I'll be okay. I promise."

"Are you sure? Your parents didn't say anything about that."

"Yeah, they did. And after the mess I caused by going off without telling anybody, do you think I'd really push the limits? No way! Dad would lock me in my room for a week!" She faked a big smile.

"Well," Doreen hesitated. "I guess that's okay. Since you'll just be downstairs. What's their phone number?"

"I have no idea. But I'll be back in an hour so you don't have to worry. Okay?"

"Well."

"Okay?"

"Okay."

"And you're here if I need you, right?" *Throw that in, make her feel needed.*

"Yes, of course," said Doreen.

"Okay, then."

"It's four fifteen now."

"I know. I'll be home at five fifteen."

Doreen took a handful of popcorn and held it. "Have fun."

"I will," said Hilary. She zipped her jacket up and spun

around. She put her hand on the doorknob.

"Oh, Hilary, wait a minute," said Doreen.

Uh-oh, she's going to call Mom and Dad at Games Galore to make sure I'm telling the truth about the hour.

But Doreen was smiling. She said, "You better make sure you have your key in case I'm in the bathroom when you get back."

Hilary grinned. "I've got it right here!" she said, and pulled the key out of her jeans pocket.

"Have fun, then," said Doreen.

Hilary waved lightly and went out, pulling the door behind her.

A few minutes later, she was out on the playground, waiting for the other members of the Cemetery Club to show up. There weren't many little kids in the playground this afternoon; it was breezy and the air was more like December than October. Gold and red leaves from nearby trees had caught on the bases of the swing sets and see-saws like baggy socks around steel ankles.

Come on, come on, come on, Hilary thought, wondering where Frank, Todd, and Audrey were. She felt kind of bad that she had lied to Doreen, but there was no other way to get away to prove herself to the three others. And she was sure a half hour wouldn't be enough time. She would be careful; she would make sure she this whole dumb club thing was done by five fifteen. And she would make sure Doreen never found out. That way, her parents wouldn't find out, either. She kicked at a clump of leaves wrapped around a spring-action hobbyhorse.

"So you showed up after all!" The shout came from the sidewalk. Hilary looked up from the leaves. The three members of the Cemetery Club were bundled up and grinning at her. Frank was in a brown coat and knitted hat, Audrey in a bright red coat with a plaid scarf, and Todd wore a gray hooded sweatshirt that was two sizes too big.

"Of course I did," Hilary said. "What'd you think?"

"We thought you'd be too scared to join our club," said Todd. He looked goofy, with the hood of his thick sweatshirt pulled and tied so tightly around his face that it seemed his face was ready to pop.

Hilary strolled over to the sidewalk. She came right up to the others to show she was ready for whatever they had in mind, even though her shoulders were starting to shiver a little.

"There's no such thing as too scared for me," she said, staring right into Todd's pop-ready face.

Audrey rolled her eyes and elbowed Frank. Frank, though, kept a stern expression on his face. He said, "Come on, then. We're going into Resurrection Cemetery."

Hilary nodded.

"Aren't you gonna call your Mommy and tell her where you'll be in case you get scared and lost and can't find your way out?"

"I don't have a phone," Hilary said, and then wished she hadn't said that. Frank didn't need to know her personal stuff. So she added, "Besides, nothing's going to scare me in there."

The four, as silent as a military parade, left the apartment complex, crossed the wide avenue, and walked down to the cemetery's entrance gate. Hilary had watched them carefully as they had gone, noticing that Frank seemed to be holding something inside his coat that he didn't want her to see.

I hope it isn't something really gross, she thought, and then gritted her teeth to prepare for whatever it was going to be. Her shoulders shivered even harder beneath her coat.

"Let's go inside," Frank said. He made a grand gesture with his arm, like a magician presenting a magic trick. "After you."

The four trooped through the entrance, Frank skipping up from behind to take the lead. They wound their way along the paved roads, between old and new sections of graves, in and out of the trees' late-afternoon shadows.

After a few more minutes, Frank took the group off the road and onto the lawn. They walked among headstones, heading toward the far side of the cemetery and a very tall, gray stone mausoleum surrounded by tall, dead grass. The trees here were old and gnarled. One had even knocked down a headstone, and it lay shattered in the weeds, as if someone had forgotten or just hadn't cared. Hilary wondered if the roots had grown down through the coffin beneath the soil. The thought made her shudder a little.

Frank saw the shudder. "Scared already, huh?" he asked.

"No," said Hilary. "Just cold is all."

Frank moved to the mausoleum and put one hand on the rough stone surface. He waved everyone else to come closer. Hilary followed Audrey and Todd. Scratchy thistles raked Hilary's jeans, making hissing, ghostly sounds. Crickets hopped in and out among the tall, dead grass.

Hilary wondered why the groundskeepers didn't do a good job in this part of the graveyard. Maybe they were scared of something.

"Sit down," said Frank. Audrey and Todd sat in the grass. Hilary put on her best "I don't care" face and said, "Are you the boss or what?"

"I'm president of the Cemetery Club. If you want to be a member you have to do what I say."

Hilary's jaw tightened. She sat in the grass.

"Audrey," said Frank, still standing. "Give me the blindfold."

Oh no! thought Hilary. *But I have to go along with it. They can't think I'm scared, no matter what!*

Audrey reached into her red coat and pulled out a red-striped man's tie. She moved over to Hilary. "I have to tie this on your eyes," she said, almost as if in an apology.

"Sure," said Hilary. "No problem."

Audrey tied the tie around Hilary's eyes, adjusting it so Hilary couldn't see. Now, with the world no longer in sight, she felt a little dizzy. But she sat still, her arms crossed in defiance.

"Now," said Frank. His voice came from above. Hilary tilted her head in the direction of the voice. "To become a member of the Cemetery Club, you have to always be brave. Nothing can make you jump or scream. Nothing can make you run away. Do you understand?"

Hilary nodded.

She heard Audrey whisper something then go quiet.

"We meet every night the two weeks before Halloween. We call up…we *summon*…ghosts, vampires, werewolves and other monsters, and there are a lot that live around here. They are terrifying. But we never are afraid. Ever. Do you understand?"

"Yep," Hilary said. A thread from the tie dangled around her nose like a spider's web and she rubbed it away.

"And sometimes," said Frank, "the ghosts and monsters follow us home. They do things to try and scare us. But anyone who shows fear gets kicked out. Do you...?"

"Yeah, yeah, okay," said Hilary, impatiently. "I understand. So what are we doing here today?"

"Initiation into the club," said Frank. "Now be quiet, and we'll call up the spirits."

Hilary drew her knees up to her chin and wrapped her arms around them. As long as they didn't do anything to hurt her, she thought. If they did, she'd quit in a second.

"We sit by the grave of Karla and Marcus Beehan," said Frank, his voice steady and serious. "They died in 1936, on the *very same day* and are buried together in this *very same stone crypt*! Yes! They were *murdered*, and they are angry! Oh, spirits of Karla and Marcus, we call you forward!"

It was the craziest thing Hilary had heard in a long time. Crazy and totally dumb. She started to giggle, a sudden, combined reaction of the jitters and the realization that this whole thing was just a lot of goofy stuff Frank and the others had made up.

Audrey said, "Be quiet, Hilary, or you'll mess it up!"

Hilary rolled her lips in between her teeth to push the giggles back down.

Frank went on in a slow, low voice. "Today we have someone who wants to be a member of our club. Karla and Marcus, you must test this person to see if she is worthy.

We want to know if she is brave enough to belong!"

"Yeah, we want to know," said Todd.

"We'll wait for a sign, Karla and Marcus," said Frank. "We'll wait for you to test this person."

Frank fell silent. No one spoke. There was no sound except the grasses rustling in the breeze, the hopping of the crickets, and the muffled sound of cars in the distance out on Archer Road.

Suddenly, Hilary felt something tickling her neck.

"Hey!" she shouted. "Stop that, Frank!"

"It's not Frank," said Todd. "No one is moving at all. You must be feeling a...*ghost*."

Yeah, right, Hilary thought, but she just tightened her jaws and waited. A few seconds later, she felt fingers on her neck, and the collar of her jacket being pulled back.

"Frank, stop it!" she snarled through her teeth.

"It's not Frank," said Audrey.

Okay, just sit still and see what...

And suddenly, there was something cold and wet and under her shirt, sliding down her skin toward her stomach. Not one something, a lot of somethings, twisting and turning and tickling.

"*Ahhh!*" Hilary cried out in disgust.

"Ha! She's scared!" shouted Frank in triumph.

"I am not scared!" Hilary shouted, rising up on her knees and shaking her jacket and the hem of her shirt to let whatever gross, gooey things on her skin fall out. "It's just cold, that's all!"

What is that? she thought in horror. *Ugh! Are they worms? I hate worms!*

"I think the ghost of Karla Beehan has put worms

down your shirt," said Frank. His voice sounded so very satisfied.

They are worms! Gross! But if I scream they'll say I failed the test!

"We told you that ghosts did scary things," said Todd. He was almost laughing.

Hilary shook her body and clawed at the worms in her shirt. Some stuck to her skin like wet paste. Finally, she peeled the last one off and tossed it away into the grass. Her hands were trembling.

"You were scared!" said Frank.

"No, of course I wasn't," said Hilary, breathing heavily. "I told you I can handle anything, even when you make stuff up, trying to pretend there are ghosts..."

And then Frank screamed, loud enough to wake the dead. Hilary ripped the blindfold from her eyes. It was hard to see for a moment; everything was bright and blurred, but she saw Frank jumping and squealing in the grass.

"Frank, what's wrong?" Audrey cried.

"Worms!" screamed Frank. He jumped to his feet and began hopping around, trying to shake something from under his jacket.

"Ha!" said Hilary. "You're the one who's scared of worms!"

"Am not!" shouted Frank. He clawed a handful of the squiggly creatures out through the neck of his jacket and threw them away. Hilary could see that these worms were strange things, not brown like earthworms but white like moonlight. Frank reached back into his jacket and got a few more. "I'm not scared, just surprised, that's all!"

Hilary, her eyes clearing, looked over at Todd and Audrey, who still sat in the grass. Their eyes were wide, their mouths hanging open.

Finally, Frank flicked the last of the white worms from his jacket and then licked his lips. He crossed his arms and frowned. He looked both furious and rattled at the same time. "I wasn't scared at all, just…just surprised. Ghosts usually only do something to one person at a time. I didn't think anything would happen to me."

"Oh, yeah, sure," said Hilary. "Like I believe that."

Audrey and Todd continued to stare.

"Well," said Frank. His mouth worked silently. It looked as though he couldn't think of what to say. It even looked like he was shaking a little. Then, finally, he found his voice, and he squared his shoulders. "I was going to do some other things today as part of the club meeting, but I think this was a really good meeting already. I mean, wow! And besides, Mom said I had to be home early because we have cousins coming to visit and I have to be there."

"What are you talking about?" asked Todd as he got to his feet.

"I said," said Frank, leaning in threateningly close to Todd and Todd stepped back a little, "I've got cousins coming. You got a problem with that?"

"No," said Todd.

Audrey stood and put her hands into her coat pockets. She looked at Frank, and then at Hilary, as if she wanted to say something, but she stayed silent.

"Then I'll see you guys later," Frank said. He stalked away and disappeared down a hillside behind the grove of tombstones.

"That's it?" Hilary asked. "That's how I get into the Cemetery Club?"

Todd turned to her. Like Frank, he looked a little uncertain about what had just happened. "That's it for now," he said. "But remember, we meet every day until Halloween. Tomorrow at six o'clock at the playground again. And since the cemetery closes at five on Saturdays, we got to climb over the fence next time. Can you do that?"

"Of course," said Hilary, not sure at all. It would be getting really dark by then. Now she wouldn't just be lying to Doreen, she'd be trespassing on private land after hours.

"And don't forget what Frank said. 'Monsters, once they're called up, can appear anytime. Anywhere.'"

"Just shut up, Todd," said Audrey. "That's enough. Let's go."

She and Todd left.

Hilary stood alone, watching them go. Her skin still crawled with the feel of the earthworms. They were so clammy and cold. "Yuck," she said to herself.

"How'd you like that?" came a voice from behind the mausoleum. Hilary turned around. Marjorie strolled around the stone side, smiling broadly. She wore the same dress she had had on when Hilary met her, this time covered with a pink sweater.

"How'd I like what? The worms one of them dropped down my shirt?" asked Hilary. "Were you watching us? I feel really stupid for freaking out like that. But I hate slimy things!"

"What does that mean, freak out?"

"You know, get really upset and yell, that kind of thing."

"You didn't freak out," said Marjorie. "You did pretty good. It was that boy, Frank, who freaked out. Ha ha ha!"

Hilary felt a giggle come up her throat. She laughed, once, and then shook her head. "I know Frank put the worms down my shirt," she said. "But who put the worms down his? Audrey?"

"No," said Marjorie. "I did it. And they weren't really worms. Look down."

Hilary looked down. There were no white worms anywhere to be seen in the grass.

"Where'd they go? Into the ground?"

"No. There weren't any worms at all. It was a trick. He just thought there were worms."

"You're kidding, right?"

"I just made him think there were worms."

"Really?"

"Yes."

"I don't get it. How did you do that?"

Marjorie smiled. It was a strange smile, one that seemed almost transparent, as if the smile didn't go all the way through to her lips. "It doesn't matter, does it?"

"Oh, I get it. Your magic's secret."

"I guess you could call it that. And it sure was funny seeing that boy hop around."

"It sure was," said Hilary. "Thanks for taking up for me."

"You're welcome." Then Marjorie looked up at the sky. "Looks like it wants to rain."

Hilary looked up, too. The late afternoon sky was heavy and gray, the clouds like thick, wet cotton. "I guess I better get on home, then," she said. "I'm betting it's close to five fifteen, anyway. And you should go home. Don't want to get that dress soaked."

Marjorie didn't nod. She just stood quietly, smiling that strange smile.

Hilary hesitated then said, "You must go to Douglas's high school. Have you met my brother at Wayne Allen High School? Douglas Wilson?"

"No," said Marjorie.

"You go to Allen High School?"

"No."

"You go to a private school?"

Marjorie shook her head.

"Oh, okay, homeschool. I get it."

"Look," said Marjorie. She pointed to the grass. Fat drops were falling and splashing. Hilary felt drips hit her head and nose. "You better go. It's going to pour. I'd hate it if my new friend caught a cold from the rain!"

Hilary looked at her watch. "Yeah, and it's almost five fifteen. So I better hurry."

Marjorie waved and walked back behind the mausoleum.

I wonder why she is still wearing the same dress I saw her in the other day? Hilary tilted her head, thinking. *Even with that sweater, she has to be cold.* Suddenly Hilary felt bad. Maybe Marjorie was homeless. Maybe she wasn't homeschooled at all because maybe she didn't even have a home. That was why she hadn't answered Hilary's question.

Hilary decided that next time she came to the cemetery, she would bring Marjorie one of her mother's old coats. It was the least she could do to thank Marjorie for coming out of nowhere to spook Frank.

Chapter 14

"Todd, I could hit you!" whispered Frank. He was in his bedroom, sitting on the edge of the bed, talking on his phone. His mother was out in the living room, working on the computer.

Todd's voice came back, loud and clear. "What? Why?"

"Putting worms down my shirt when I was trying to scare Hilary! I'm so mad at you!"

"Hey, cut it out!" said Todd. "I didn't put anything down your dumb shirt!"

"Don't lie to me!" Then Frank lowered his voice. The last thing he needed was for his mother to hear him talking about pranks on people. He'd been grounded for three days last year for scaring an old lady with a large rubber spider the day before Halloween.

"I'm not lying!" said Todd.

"Then Audrey did it! I'm going to call her and tell her a thing or two!"

"Frank, be quiet and listen to me. Nobody put worms down your shirt! I'm not lying!"

Frank sat back, hard, against the pillows on the bed. He didn't say anything for a moment. He could hear Todd's angry breathing through the phone.

“You didn’t put worms down my shirt,” he said finally. It wasn’t a question.

“No!” said Todd. “I promise you that!”

“And Audrey didn’t, either.”

“No! I told you. I don’t know what happened. Maybe you put them down your own shirt to make it all seem more real to Hilary. Or maybe they fell out of the tree.”

Frank thought about this. Maybe they did fall out of the tree beside the mausoleum. Though he’d never, ever seen worms like that before. And wasn’t it so creepy, that they would wait and fall out of the tree and worm him right after Hilary had gotten wormed? Almost like it was planned.

“Whatever, dude,” said Frank. “Never mind. It was just worms. No big deal. Now I got to go. My pizza’s getting cold.”

“You like cold pizza.”

“Yeah, and I’m tired of talking to you.”

Frank pushed the red “END” button on the phone and dropped the phone onto the bed. He looked down at the pattern of the rug. Okay, Todd and Audrey didn’t do the worms. He believed Todd was telling the truth. And Hilary didn’t do the worms.

So they *had* to have dropped out of the tree. That was all there was to it. But the worms were so weird looking. They looked more like ghosts of worms than real, live worms.

And he sure didn’t believe in ghosts.

Chapter 15

Saturday morning, while Hilary was in the kitchen eating cereal, her father came in and said, "Your mom's not going with me to the store today. She's not feeling well and so Douglas is going to take her to the doctor in a little bit."

"Oh, no," said Hilary, a familiar rock of worry turning in her chest. "Poor Mom. I thought she was doing better."

Her father tried to smile, but the smile was tired. "I'd like you to be especially attentive of Mom today."

"I..."

"She needs you. She needs us."

"I know, but..." Hilary swallowed a bite of cereal. She had planned on asking her dad to drop her off at the bookstore on his way to the game store. It was only three blocks, so it shouldn't be a big deal for her to go there and then walk home alone. It was broad daylight, after all, not late afternoon when it would start to get dark and her parents would think she needed a...

Babysitter, she thought sourly.

"Okay, Hilary?"

With the money she'd saved from allowances, she wanted to see if there was a book she could buy on local ghosts. If she was going to fight fire with fire when it came to the Cemetery Club, the more she knew about local hauntings and legends, the better. And she had to stand up to Frank, Todd, and Audrey and beat them at their own game!

"Hilary, are you listening to me?"

"I'm listening."

"Okay."

"But…when is she supposed to be back from the doctor?"

Mr. Wilson found his coat on the back of a kitchen chair. He slipped it on then pulled his gloves from the pocket. "It doesn't really matter, does it, Sweetie? The appointment is at nine thirty. It could be an hour, maybe two, maybe longer. What is so important that you can't be here to do some things Mom would do if she was home and feeling better?"

"I wanted you to drop me off at the bookstore."

"Do you need something for school?"

"Well, no."

"Then you don't need to go today. It can wait."

"But I want to go look at books for a little while. I really need to get a book."

"It can wait. Why not go this evening? I'll go with you. I enjoy bookstores as much as you do."

"I need to go before tonight."

"Why?"

I can't tell Dad about the Cemetery Club! "Dad, you know I love Mom and I want her to be well and I want to help but…"

"But what?"

"But," she blurted out, "why do things always have to stop 'cause of her? I'm not asking for anything major!"

"Hilary!"

Hilary's stomach suddenly hurt. She was angry and sad and frustrated, and she didn't know how to make all those bad feelings go away. She blurted out, "Back in Pennsylvania I couldn't go out with my friends lots of times because I had to stay with Mom when she was sick. We moved to Illinois because Mom needed a job that let her sit down a lot. That was supposed to make things better for everybody."

Mr. Wilson's mouth opened and then closed, as if he was too shocked to speak. Finally, he said in a strained, cold voice, "If you want to go to the bookstore, fine. Do whatever you want, Hilary. Don't let us ruin your plans."

He stormed out of the apartment.

Douglas came into the kitchen. "What was that all about?" he asked.

Hilary didn't want her cereal anymore. She got up and washed it down the disposal. "Nothing," she said. "I'm going to the bookstore. I'll be back by eleven, before you and Mom get home. Don't worry, I'll get the dishes done and the rooms vacuumed."

She found her coat, counted to sixty to make sure her father would be gone from the parking lot, and then went downstairs and out into the fresh October morning.

It wouldn't take much more than five minutes to walk to the store. Maybe by then, she hoped, she wouldn't be crying anymore.

Chapter 16

Frank was up earlier than usual for a Saturday morning. He had plans to make. Yesterday, the worm trick hadn't done what he'd hoped it would. For some weird reason it had all turned against him instead of scaring Hilary. Tonight, though, the club would meet when it was nice and dark. They would sneak into the cemetery and there would be something to scare the socks off old Hilary Wilson!

What he needed was to download a bunch of creepy sounds off the computer and onto an MP3 player. Audrey had a good one, and a set of little speakers, too, small enough to fit into his coat pockets and then hide in the deep cemetery grass and not be seen. He would play the scary sounds, which would help set the stage for whatever else he would come up with.

He'd called Audrey a few minutes ago, waking her up, and she wearily agreed to let him use the player, but added he'd have to come get it from her house.

With his coat over his arm, he pulled his apartment door shut and walked out of the main door. He paused on the front steps, stretching and yawning. Then he put his coat on, rechecked to see that his apartment key was in the pocket, and then hopped down the steps.

Then he stopped.

There was Hilary Wilson, her back to Frank, walking across the parking lot between the cars, heading away from the building. Frank wondered where she was going, but that really didn't matter. What mattered was that he now had another chance to scare her.

Quietly, Frank bent down and followed Hilary.

Chapter 17

Hilary glanced across the four lanes of traffic on Archer as she walked along the street, heading west toward Justice Books and Café. Through the rushing cars, she could see the Resurrection Cemetery and its long stretch of iron fencing.

Then she stopped.

Marjorie, in her white dress and a yellow scarf, was standing outside the cemetery fence, waving at a car as it slowed down beside her. Smiling, Marjorie opened the car door and hopped in.

"Don't do that!" Hilary shouted across the sea of rumbling vehicles. "It's dangerous to hitchhike!" But Marjorie didn't hear. The car into which she'd climbed pulled away from the curb.

I hope nothing bad happens to her! Hilary thought. *I can't believe she is doing something so thoughtless!*

Hilary watched the car as it was swallowed up in the moving traffic.

Next time I see her, I'm going to tell her she has to be careful. If she's being homeschooled, her mom or dad might be teaching her lots of good stuff, but they sure didn't teach her to hitchhike! I don't want my friend to get hurt.

"Yeah, Hilary," she muttered. "Listen to yourself. It's not like you always do what your parents say to do, either, or not do what they say not to do."

Hilary wiped away some remaining tears, turned and walked on, crossing the graveled parking lot of the Melody Lounge, and headed to the bookstore. "Guess I've found at least one friend here in Illinois," she said aloud. "I just hope my friend is safe."

Chapter 18

Frank hid behind cars when he thought Hilary was going to turn around, but she only did once, and that was to look across Archer Road. Most of the time, she walked with her hands in her pockets and her face straight ahead.

He'd collected gravel as he'd followed Hilary, putting the pieces into his pockets. He was waiting for the right time to use them.

Frank didn't care anymore about scaring little kids around the neighborhood. Scaring little kids was kid's stuff. Hilary was a challenge. It would take a lot to scare her. And whatever it took, Frank was going to do it.

Hilary crossed in front of the Melody Lounge and walked along the barren stretch of land beside it. Frank tiptoed quickly after, dipping behind a street-side bench when he thought she heard him. Still, she didn't turn around.

Now! he thought.

He pulled a rock from his pocket and hurled it at Hilary. It hit the ground by her foot. She slowed her stride, looked down where the rock hit, and kept on walking.

Frank hurled another rock. It struck Hilary in the back. She whirled around, frowning. Frank pulled down farther behind the bench and peeked through the wood slats of the bench's back. He put his hand over his mouth so he wouldn't laugh out loud.

Hilary looked back and forth, then turned and began walking again.

Frank followed and then dove behind a small tree. He took a few rocks from his pocket and flung them at Hilary. They hit her shoulder and the back of her head. She spun around and shouted, "Who's doing that?"

Frank held as still as he could, even though his shoulders shook from his giggling.

"I mean it! Who is that?" shouted Hilary.

Frank didn't move.

Hilary looked all around, her expression showing more and more worry when she couldn't find a source for the rocks. "I'll call the cops, just you wait!"

Frank smirked. He knew she didn't have a phone.

Hilary turned, then, and began walking. Very fast. She passed the gas station, muffler shop, and paint store.

Frank hurried from behind the tree. He moved along in the shadows of the buildings and in and out between the parked cars, staying low and silent. He jumped behind a brown station wagon and hurled a handful of rocks at Hilary, who was gaining ground. Some hit her, some landed on the ground at her side.

Hilary turned around and came back several yards. Frank, seeing her come through the windows of the car, lay down and rolled beneath the vehicle.

"Who are you?" Hilary demanded, her voice quivering.

Good, Frank thought. *She's really creeped out now!*

"Whoever you are, you stop that right now! I've had it!

I'll tell the police I'm being bothered!"

No, you won't. You don't have a phone. You told me that already.

"I mean it!"

There was a moment of silence, and Hilary walked on. From ground level, Frank could see her blue sneakers trotting away. He lay there, enjoying his success, then rolled out from under the car.

He got up. A woman with a can of paint in her hands stood staring at him from the door of the store. He shrugged, and said, "My dog got away. I thought he was under the car."

"Hmmm," said the woman, her nose twitching and her eyes pinched in distrust. She brushed past Frank and climbed into her car.

Frank watched her drive out onto Archer Road then he looked at his phone and saw the time. He was supposed to be at Audrey's already, getting the player and speakers.

He hurried around the paint store and cut across the rear delivery driveway. He climbed a sagging wire fence and dropped down into the tall grasses of a vacant lot. This was a short cut to Audrey's. Her house was only five blocks away this way. Frank put his hands into his pockets, stretched his neck back, and began to whistle.

A small rock struck him on the neck.

He stopped and turned back. There was no one to be seen.

"Who's that?" he called.

It has to be Hilary! he thought. He looked all around. There was no sound, no movement. And, there was no place anyone could hide. This lot was really big, and there was only grass and thistles. No trees.

But it can't be Hilary.

Frank's heart began to pound. Hilary had gone down Archer Road, he'd seen her. There was no way she could have come back this fast with rocks to hide and throw at him from as far back at the paint store. She would have to be a professional pitcher to do that!

Slowly, Frank turned and began walking across the lot again.

He listened for a second set of footsteps. He only heard his own.

Suddenly, small rocks came flying at him from everywhere. A shower of pebbles, black, gray, and white, hit him from all sides, his front, his back, from above, showering him like hailstones. Frank yelled and began to run, but couldn't outrun the rocks. They hit his arms, his hands, his face, his legs.

Pock, ping, thud, thump!

He couldn't turn to see where they were coming from, but his mind screamed at him, *They're coming from everywhere!*

"Stop it!" he wailed. "Leave me alone!"

The rocks kept coming. Frank tripped and went down in the grass then pushed himself back up and kept running. The shower of pebbles kept up with him.

Ping, pock, thump, thud!

"Oww!" Frank cried. Ahead, through the flying rocks that swarmed around him like flies, he could see the other side of the lot and the wire fence. He narrowed his eyes to slits and ran for the fence. His hands came in contact with the wire; he threw one leg over it. His body went up and over. He landed on the ground on his back. He closed his eyes and covered his face with his arms.

The rock shower stopped. Frank slowly moved his arms and opened his eyes. Above, the morning sky was bright and blue. Clouds were fluffy and as white as unflavored snow-cone ice.

He stood up, panting hard. He looked back over the fence at the vacant lot. There was no way anyone could have thrown those rocks at him. It was not humanly possible. But then, he noticed something really strange. He could see none of the rocks. There should have been piles of rocks all over the place, but there were none.

Frank touched his arms. He could felt deep bruises forming and thick welts rising beneath his sleeves. He could feel blood flowing down his face from the deep scratches. He reached up to wipe the blood away.

But there was no blood. He wiped his face harder and his fingers still came away with no blood. He shrugged out of his coat, pushed up his shirt sleeves, and found no bruises, no welts. As if the whole thing had been nothing but an illusion. As if he'd just imagined it.

Not possible, he thought. *I was attacked, I know it! But where are the bruises? Where are the rocks?*

It took a while before he stopped shaking enough to go to Audrey's house for the player.

Chapter 19

Mrs. Wilson had been checked by the doctor and some tests were scheduled for the following week. Hilary spent most of the afternoon with her, preparing home-made spaghetti sauce, hanging up framed pictures in the living room, putting away dishes, and trying to be encouraging. Mrs. Wilson didn't have the energy to do much, so she curled up on the sofa with a blanket to take a nap. As much as Hilary had complained to her father, this time alone with her mother was quiet, comfortable, and nice.

And so she felt awful, lying yet again.

Hilary sat on the chair near her mother and handed her a cup of hot tea. Then she said, "Can I go watch movies in Frank's apartment after supper? You know Frank. He's in my class at school and his mom's the apartment manager. Douglas'll be home by dinnertime. And Dad'll be back soon after that."

"Sure," said Hilary's mother with a tired but kind smile. "And thanks for all you did for me today."

Hilary gave her mom a hug and held it for many seconds. She wished her hug could cure her mom once and for all. She wished it would make everything better, for all of them.

When dinnertime came around, Hilary tried not to eat too fast. She wanted to seem like everything was calm and normal, and not that she was getting ready to face down some smarty-pants who wanted to prove they could scare her. She finished before Douglas and her mother, then got up and took her coat from the closet. "See you guys later," she said. "I'm going to watch movies with my friends."

Douglas got up and walked her to the apartment door. "So, you've got some friends now?" he asked.

Hilary could tell by his voice that he didn't really believe her. Douglas was smart. He knew she wasn't telling the whole truth about where she was going, but he didn't ask her anything more.

"That's what I said, isn't it?"

"Hilary, please don't do anything dumb."

Hilary hesitated, then said, "Of course I won't. Gee, thanks for the confidence."

Then she moved around him and out of the apartment.

Fifteen minutes later, four seventh graders crossed Archer Road in the growing darkness and walked down the sidewalk beside the cemetery. Hilary wished she had brought a flashlight, but she didn't know if the Cemetery Club allowed it. She wondered how dark a cemetery could really get at night. Beneath her jacket, her body trembled.

Frank seemed strangely tense tonight. He kept glancing over his shoulders as if he thought something was going to hit him. It made Hilary think back on the morning, when someone had hurled rocks at her. At first, she'd been scared. She had remembered what Frank had said about ghosts hanging around once you call them up.

But then, she had laughed at herself. There were no such things as ghosts, of course, especially no ghosts that threw rocks at people on the street. Hilary had figured it had been either Todd or Frank. She didn't think it was Audrey. Even though Audrey hung out with Frank and Todd, she seemed to be a little nicer than the other two. She seemed to enjoy scary stories more than the idea of scaring someone else.

"We don't need to go all the way down to the main gate," said Frank as they walked. "It's locked up by now for sure. But in just a second we'll see a tree on the inside of the fence, right up against it. We'll give each other a boost up the fence, then climb onto the tree limb and drop down into the cemetery."

"Okay," the others said, almost in unison.

They walked on another minute.

"There it is," Frank said quietly, pointing at a bare maple tree just inside the fence. One curved, thick branch almost touched the top of the wrought iron.

One at a time, when they were pretty sure no one on the street was watching, Frank boosted the others up the side of the fence and onto the branch. Audrey went first, Hilary second, and Todd next. Then Todd leaned down to grab Frank's hand and the boy scrambled up until he could get a leg over the branch.

All four dropped down silently into the dark, shadowy cemetery where leaves spun in the wind and faint moonlight pooled about the dead grasses like spilled, spoiled milk.

Chapter 20

Frank had a couple things hiding in his coat. Tonight, he would prove to the others what a baby Hilary Wilson really was. Tonight, as he told Todd and Audrey, he would *win*!

Earlier in the afternoon, Frank had taken the player and speaker he'd borrowed from Audrey and hidden them beneath a pile of fallen leaves behind a large angel statue in the "C" section of the cemetery. He'd made sure the batteries were working. He'd compiled terrifying sounds from online, complete with chains clanking, doors slamming, groans, moans, and shrieks. The sounds were perfect, and they even made the hair on his arms stand up when he played them back to make sure it was ready.

As the four walked through the darkness, Frank patted the pocket on the inside of his coat and grinned at what he knew would be an extra scare for Hilary.

He had a jar full of spiders.

Oh, it had taken him a while to collect them all. He'd gone down into the laundry room and rounded up a few. He'd called Todd and Audrey, but only Todd agreed to find some and bring them for the jar. Audrey said she thought that might be dangerous to scare someone with spiders. “I like to get scared,” she said, “but I don’t want to do something that might get somebody hurt.”

Frank had said, “Thanks for nothing.”

But between him and Todd, they had come up with over twenty. None were really dangerous to people, he was pretty sure. Most were small, dusty brown spiders but four were large black-and-yellow spiders with long, sleek legs, found clinging to their intricate webs in the bushes behind the apartment playground.

Clouds moved in and out in front of the moon; night birds made strange, chittering noises in the trees.

Audrey said, “I hope this isn’t much farther,” she said. “It’s pretty cold out here tonight.”

“That’s your problem,” said Frank. “Should have worn a hat.”

“Shhh,” said Todd. “We might scare the spooks away.”

They hiked on across the huge, silent cemetery, past countless gravestones, trees, and mausoleums. And then, Frank spotted the “C” marker at an intersection. He went off the road, between tall markers and short, looking for the angel. She was a very pretty angel, with long wings and flowing dress carved out of marble. There were a lot of angels in this cemetery, but this one seemed to be looking at him as he’d passed it earlier in the afternoon. Maybe she thought it would be fun to watch Hilary Wilson get scared. So Frank decided this would be a good place to have the club’s second meeting.

They sat in a circle in the scratchy grass at the foot

of the angel, Frank closest to it to make sure the remote would reach. He put his hand down and crawled it around the stone base of the angel to make sure the player and speakers had not been found and stolen. They were still there. He sighed with relief.

"Okay," Frank said, speaking low, slow, and menacingly, "we meet again for the Cemetery Club. Tonight, we are at the grave of Robert Richardson. He *died* and was *buried* in 1943." He emphasized the words "died" and "buried," hoping to set the scene just right. "We are going to call up his spirit like we called up the spirits of Karla and Marcus yesterday."

"But their spirits didn't do anything," said Hilary.

Frank glared at her. It was hard to see her face in the dark, but he bet she was smiling and rolling her eyes like she had back in English class. It made him angry, but he tried not to get angry back. He had to stay in control. "Oh, yes they did," he said.

"You mean worms down my shirt? That was you and you know it."

"Like worms down shirts, yet," Frank said. "And like other mysterious things that might have haunted you or any one of us this morning."

"Like what, rocks hitting my back? That was you, or Todd. Good try, but it didn't scare me at all."

Frank felt the skin on the top of his head tighten. *Yes,* he thought. *Like rocks. Like rocks that someone or something threw at me this morning. But I'm not telling anyone about that!*

"Be quiet," said Frank. "We have to be quiet so I can call up Robert."

"Pffft," said Hilary.

"Do you understand?" Frank demanded.

Todd and Audrey nodded, but Hilary just sat with her arms crossed.

Chapter 21

Whatever they do, Hilary thought, *I won't get scared. The worms yesterday were pretty bad, and the rocks this morning were mean, but none were really scary. Tonight I won't scream or run away no matter what! I have to prove to them I'm strong and brave!* She rubbed her arms to get rid of chills that seemed determined to make her shiver.

Frank groaned, waggled his head and waved his arms, then started chanting to get the spirit of Robert Richardson to come out.

"Ooooooh whooooo wheeeee doooooo looooo!"

Hilary glanced at Todd and Audrey. They were listening intently. She looked back at Frank, watching to see if his waving hands held any worms.

"Zoooooo loooooo ahhhhhhh noooooooo waaaaaaaa!" chanted Frank. The sound dug in Hilary's ear like a bug.

Suddenly, Hilary heard someone whisper her name. She looked again at Todd and Audrey. They were still watching Frank. Neither one of them had called her, and it didn't seem like they'd heard the voice.

"We call you, Richard, to come forward to us!" said Frank. He lowered his hands and put them into his pockets. He lifted his chin and said, "We're waiting for you!"

The whisper came again. Hilary's name on the air from somewhere behind. Hilary glanced over her shoulder. In the night shadows, crouching beside a bush, was Marjorie.

Hilary shook her head a little held her finger to her lips. But then Marjorie whispered, "Don't worry. They can't hear me."

Hilary mouthed, "Why not?"

"Just because," said Marjorie. "Trust me."

"Lightning, thunder, terror, fear, ghost of Richard, come right here!" wailed Frank. Hilary looked at him. His head was thrown back and his eyes were closed.

"Want me to help?" Marjorie whispered.

Hilary glanced back again. "How?" she mouthed.

"I know a few magic tricks, like the worms yesterday. Do you want to scare that boy really good?"

Hilary nodded slightly so the others wouldn't notice.

Frank stopped chanting. He picked up sticks from the ground and snapped them into little pieces. He piled the pieces up in front of him.

"These sticks represent the fire of eternity. We'll light it and the cold, dead spirit of Robert will come forth to the warmth. Ooooooh whoooooo!"

Hilary looked back to see what Marjorie thought of all this, but Marjorie was gone.

Weird. She comes and goes awfully fast without making a sound.

"Audrey!" said Frank with a snap of his fingers. "Do you have the eternity light?"

Audrey handed Frank a match and he struck the tip on the side of Robert's angel. He lowered the match to the pile of sticks. After a moment of smoking, the sticks caught fire. Todd leaned over and blew on them. The fire grew to nearly a foot.

"I'm sure it's against the law to have a fire in the cemetery," said Hilary.

"Yeah, and it's against the law to climb the fence into the cemetery when it's closed, too. So be quiet!" said Todd.

"Fire of eternity," chanted Frank, "bring forth the spirit of Robert Richardson! We want him to come and tell us how he died!"

And then, from somewhere nearby, Hilary heard the soft sound of moaning. It wasn't from Todd, Frank, or Audrey. It seemed to come from behind the angel, somewhere back in the darkness. She caught her breath. Her heart skipped a beat.

"What's that?" she asked, but Frank answered, "Shhh!"

The sounds came more loudly now; the moaning mixed with hissing, like wind over the beach, like a snake through leaves.

Hilary looked again at the other kids. None of them were making the sounds. Her mind scrambled to figure out what was going on.

The hissing and groaning turned into agonized wails.

Chapter 22

Ha, I've got her really scared this time! Frank thought. *And out here in the cemetery, the sounds are even creepier than they were back at my apartment!*

Audrey and Todd sat without moving, watching Hilary and the little fire. Hilary didn't say anything, but he could see the sounds had her spooked because her eyes were growing wider by the moment.

When I hear the right thing on the recording, I'll stomp out the fire and then...then the spiders!

Chapter 23

The wailing made the hair on Hilary's arms prickle and her mouth to go dry. *Stop it,* she told herself, *there's just somebody else in the cemetery, somebody out in the dark behind that angel, someone Frank talked into hiding and making noises. That has to be it. That has to be what's…*

But following the screams were the sounds of clanging, banging, doors creaking and slamming, and loud, haunted bells tolling loudly.

Hey, wait! There aren't any doors near here.

"Robert, hear me!" wailed Frank.

Okay, I get it! Frank recorded sounds to try and scare me. What a joke!

"Robert! Come to us!"

This is so fake! Hilary thought. *How dumb do they think I am? But wait. If I pretend to think it's real, that will prove I'm as brave as anybody else. It will prove I'm good enough to be in the Cemetery Club!*

"Robert!" said Frank. "Tell us how you died!"

And then, there came a low, muffled voice mixed in with the other frightful sounds. "I was killed!" it said. "My brother murdered me! He put spiders in my bed at night, poisonous spiders! And they bit me to death!"

Suddenly, Frank jumped to his feet, his eyes bright as coal chips in the glow of the little fire, an ominous grin on his face. He held up a jar full of...what? Hilary couldn't see very well.

"Like this?" shouted Frank.

The voice hissed, "Yessssss!"

Frank lowered the jar to the light of the fire so Hilary could see clearly. It was full of spiders, crawling frantically over each other, some furry and small, others huge with long, pointed legs and fat, shiny bodies.

"Oh!" cried Hilary.

"Spiders like *this*!" Frank shouted. And then, he stomped on the little fire, kicking flame out. Darkness came on them as suddenly as someone pulling a black curtain across the world.

"I've opened the jar, Hilary, and dumped the spiders at your feet!" said Frank. "They're out! They're coming for you, just like they came for *Robert*!"

Hilary scooted backward, gasping, wondering if they were really out and how fast they could crawl and if they were really poisonous.

"They're coming!" shouted Frank. "They crawl really fast!"

Hilary scooted farther away, her back coming in contact with a rough tombstone behind her, preventing her from moving any more. So she scrambled to her feet. "No!" she shouted, slapping at her legs to keep any spiders from crawling up her jeans.

Frank began to giggle. Todd began to giggle. Audrey began to giggle, too.

They got me! This was a trick to make me freak out and I did! I showed how scared I was! I hate this!

"Ha, ha!" laughed Frank. "I didn't really dump the spiders out. But you screamed just like a baby! You failed the test!"

But then the muffled voice behind the angel said, "There are no spiders in your jar. There never were any spiders in your jar."

Frank stopped laughing. Todd stopped laughing. Frank said, "Hey, what's going on? Who's that?"

"Look in the jar, Frank," said the voice. "You'll see what I'm talking about."

Frank fumbled with something, then snapped on a small flashlight. The beam was narrow and faint. The flashlight shook in Frank's hand.

"Who's that?" Frank managed. "Who's talking?"

"Look in the jar, Frank," came the voice. "They aren't any spiders in there. They've gone somewhere else!"

Frank trained the flashlight's beam on the jar, which was now lying on the ground at his feet, the lid still secured. Hilary stepped closer to see. So did Audrey and Todd. The jar was totally empty. The spiders had vanished.

"They were in there a second ago," said Audrey.

Todd frowned. "I saw them, too. What happened to them?"

"I…I don't know," managed Frank.

"And who…" began Todd, "who was that talking? That didn't sound like you, Frank."

"It *wasn't* me!" said Frank.

"You're such a cheat!" said Hilary with disgust. "I know that now. You recorded spooky sounds and you recorded your voice and tried to disguise it so I wouldn't know it. What a stupid Cemetery Club! Everything's fake!"

"But you saw them, Hilary! I know you did!" shouted Frank.

"I don't know what I saw. Maybe I only thought I did," said Hilary.

"But if you want spiders," said the low, mumbled voice from behind the angel, "here are some for you!"

Suddenly, spiders began to crawl out of Frank's hair. Small, furry, brown spiders. Big, sleek spiders with black and orange stripes. Fat black spiders with impossibly long legs.

Audrey, Hilary, Todd, and Frank all screamed at the same time. The flashlight flew from Frank's grasp and Hilary caught it. She turned it around quickly and shined it on Frank as spiders scurried down his forehead, cheeks, and chin. Some disappeared into the collar of his jacket. Frank slapped his face and chest. He jumped up and down. More spiders came out of his hair, dropping to the tip of his nose, scrambling over his lips, around and down his neck.

"Help help help!" Frank cried. He jumped and slapped and screamed.

"Get them off me! Help me!"

And then all the spiders disappeared. Just as suddenly as they had appeared, they vanished.

"Hey," said Audrey. "They're gone!"

"No they aren't, there's still all over me!" shouted Frank. He continued to slap his head and his chest, continued to jump up and down in an attempt to shake out any that had gone into his clothes.

"No, really, Frank!" said Todd. "They aren't there any more."

Frank shook some more then felt down his shirt. "Hey, there really aren't any," he said. Then he reached into his hair and raked his fingers back and forth. "None there, either."

"Did we imagine the spiders?" asked Audrey. "All of us at the same time?"

"I don't know," said Todd with a visible shiver.

"And...whose voice was that on the recording?" asked Audrey, her hands clasped nervously beneath her chin. "That second voice sure wasn't yours, Frank."

"Recording!" said Hilary. "I knew it! You recorded scary sounds and then that ridiculous voice, talking about how Richard was killed by poisonous spiders!"

Audrey stepped around the angel and came back with a small MP3 player and pair of speakers. She tapped the player with her forefinger and the recording came back on. It started with the moans, the doors slamming, the bells clanging, and the hissing. And, then the voice came back on. "I was killed! My brother murdered me! He put spiders in my bed at night, poisonous spiders! And they bit me to death!"

"Yep!" said Hilary. "It's *your* voice, Frank! I knew it all along!"

"Shh, now, listen for the next part!" said Audrey. "Where the voice says there really are no spiders in the jar."

And then there was a loud voice, coming from the player, speaking loudly and clearly. But it wasn't a repeat of what it said earlier. Instead, the voice chided, "Frank!

Do you think you can stop what you started? When you call up ghosts, you're going to get ghosts! You said so, yourself! Ha ha ha ha ha!"

Audrey flinched and dropped the player to the ground.

The voice continued, "By the way, how'd you like the little rock shower this morning? You couldn't outrun it, could you?"

"NO!" shouted Frank. He stamped on the player, snapping it in two.

"Hey! That was my player!" shouted Audrey.

"Hilary did it!" said Frank. He pointed a trembling finger at Hilary. His face was tight with rage and fear. "She did it! I don't know how she did it, but she did!"

"I didn't do anything, Frank!" said Hilary.

"Oh yes, you did! That's the only answer. You think you're so ahead of the game! You figured out how to play tricks on me…on us! You figured some way to make me think I had spiders all over me! And you must have come out this afternoon and recorded all that other stuff!"

"I did not!"

"Somehow you made it look like all the spiders in my jar…" Frank snatched the flashlight from Hilary, picked up the jar and shined the light on it. The spiders were there, inside the glass, crawling over one another.

"They're back!" said Todd.

"I think they were always there!" said Frank. "Hilary did it! Some kind of stupid magic trick from some stupid magic book, I bet! That's not fair, playing tricks like that!"

"Not fair?" said Hilary. "Look who's talking! You recorded stupid sounds hoping to scare me! You had a jar with spiders and tried to make me think you'd dumped them out to crawl on me and bite me! Well, I might have been scared. But when we saw spiders on your head, Audrey was scared, too. So was Todd. And so were *you*! You were more scared than any of us!"

Frank stepped up to Hilary. She could feel the fury in his voice before she even heard it. "I don't know how you did what you did, but you just wait! You don't know what you're in for at the next meeting!"

"Don't try any more tricks!" growled Hilary, nose to nose with Frank.

"And you don't, either!" Frank snarled back.

"I've had enough of this!" said Hilary. "I'm going home!"

"Fine," said Frank. "Go! But you haven't seen the half of it! Club meeting adjourned!"

Chapter 24

Frank lay in his bed, staring up at the ceiling. How in the world did Hilary do it? How did she make the spiders disappear, and then make everybody think he had spiders crawling out of his hair? Did she have other people helping her, people he didn't know about?

"Or wait!" he said aloud. "Did Audrey and Todd join up with her to turn on me? No, they wouldn't do that, would they? They're my friends!"

The day had been terrible, and terrifying. Rocks coming at him from nowhere in the morning. Then, in the cemetery, the voice on the tape, taunting him. And scariest of all…the spiders!

He turned over and looked at the little clock on his nightstand. It was 1:05 a.m. *I'll never get to sleep*, he thought. He reached over and picked up the spider jar from beside the clock. The spiders had been a great idea. But how, how did they…?

"Agh!" Frank cried. He let go of the jar and it shattered on the floor beside his bed. Something was crawling up his hand, up his wrist. Something with little tickly legs on his arm.

He brushed his arm, jumped up, and ran to the light

switch. He flicked it on.

There, on the floor where he'd knocked it off, was an upside-down stinkbug.

Frank stared at it, sighed, and then scooped it up. He opened his window, unlatched the screen, and set the stinkbug free. "Get out of here, bug. At least you aren't a spider."

He got back into bed and pulled the covers up around him. "I'm not going to let this bother me," he whispered. "Nobody's going to get the best of me. I know all about spooks and ghosts. I know they aren't real. I'm going to figure out ways to scare Hilary so bad she'll wish she'd never even moved here!"

In bed, Hilary stared at the ceiling, unable to sleep. A lot of things were on her mind. She had lied again to her mother when she said she'd had a good time at the movie with her new friends.

Friends? thought Hilary. *What a joke! I have no friends, and I'm lying and sneaking around trying to prove how brave I am. I'm not brave. I'm afraid Audrey and Frank and Todd will think I'm a coward, so I'm doing things I shouldn't do, which means I really am a coward!*

Hilary thought of her mother's face, how it seemed to relax with happiness when she thought Hilary was finally fitting in. She thought of her father, who had apologized when he got home from work for being impatient with her, but he'd been working hard and he was tired. He said he promised to try to be a better dad. She thought of Douglas, and how he urged her to be careful, even when she knew he suspected her sneakings.

You're a great mom, Mom, Hilary thought. *You're a great dad, Dad. And you're a great brother, Douglas. I've been lying to you. I've been bratty. And I really sorry!*

But…

But she had to keep sneaking, at least for a little while. She had to make it through Halloween. She couldn't back down now. Then, after Halloween, she could hold her head up against Audrey, Todd, and Frank and anybody else who might give her trouble. And then, after Halloween, she'd never lie to her parents again.

"I won't, I promise!" she whispered into the darkness.

Hilary rolled over and stared at the wall.

It was Marjorie, she though suddenly. It was Marjorie who had done the tricks that had scared Frank so badly. Marjorie had somehow made the spiders disappear and then reappear in Frank's hair. Somehow, she had gotten her voice onto Frank's recording. Hilary couldn't figure how, but those were some really amazing magic tricks.

Maybe, Hilary thought, *I'll invite Marjorie home with me this week, if I can find her. We can plan some new tricks and I can be part of them next time.*

"And after Halloween," Hilary said quietly, "it will all be over with." She pulled her blanket up under her chin. "And I'm glad! I can't wait for this to all be over."

Chapter 25

Mrs. Wilson, who had gone to work with Mr. Wilson Sunday afternoon because she said she was feeling much better, called from the game store. Hilary was in the living room flipping through her new book on ghosts when the phone rang.

"Hilary," her mother said. "Your dad and I decided to close the store early tonight. We're taking you and Douglas out to eat. It's been a long time since we've done something like that and we thought it'd be fun!"

"Um," said Hilary. The Cemetery Club met tonight at five! "Well..."

"Well?" said her mother. "Are you okay? Do you want to go?"

Douglas came into the living room. He was barefoot and dressed in jeans and a sweatshirt. He was rubbing his wet hair with a towel, making it stand up like bristles.

"Who's on the phone?" he asked.

"Mom," said Hilary.

"Is everything okay?"

"Yeah," said Hilary. "They want to take us out to eat tonight."

Douglas smiled. He leaned over and said into the

phone, "Great! That sounds like fun. We haven't been out to eat together since we left Pennsylvania!"

On the other end of the line, Mrs. Wilson said "Wonderful! Why don't you and Hilary be ready and we will pick you up at 5:30?"

"Sure," said Douglas. "Oh, would you mind if I invited Yvonne?"

"That would be fine, Douglas," said Mrs. Wilson. "We've been wanting to meet her."

"'Bye, then," said Douglas.

"'Bye," said Hilary. She hung up the phone.

"What's the matter, Hilary?" asked Douglas. He dropped down onto the loveseat and continued to rub at his hair. "Don't you want to go out to eat?"

"Yeah," she said. "It'll be fine." *It won't be fine*, she thought. *We're supposed to meet tonight. They're going to think I chickened out. They're going to think they won!*

"Then cheer up," Douglas said. "We'll have a good time. And I want you to meet Yvonne, too. She's really nice. You'll like her."

Yvonne was Douglas's new girlfriend. She was a senior at Wayne Allen High School. She and Doug talked on the phone a lot when Doug got home at night.

"Yeah," said Hilary. She reached for the remote control and turned on the television. She flipped through several channels. Football. Fishing. News. Some reality show with people digging through abandoned storage units. Football. A black-and-white movie. She turned it off and tossed the remote control to Douglas. "Here," she said. "Maybe you can find something you like."

There was a knock on the door. Hilary hopped up

and peeked through the peephole. It was Audrey. Hilary pulled the door open.

Audrey stood in the hallway, hands in the pockets of her red coat. "Hi," she said.

"Hi," said Hilary. What in the world was she doing here? Was this a Cemetery Club trick?

"I didn't know your phone number," she said quietly, "so I came on over here."

"Okay," said Hilary hesitantly.

"I just wanted to tell you that I'm quitting the club," said Audrey. "It's stupid and I'm out."

"What do you mean, it's stupid? I thought you really liked it."

"Why don't you invite her in," called Douglas from the loveseat. "Don't make anyone stand out in the hall, Hilary, it's rude."

"Want to come in?" asked Hilary.

"No, thanks," said Audrey. "But I did want to talk to you just for a minute."

"Okay."

"Like I said, I'm quitting. And it doesn't have anything to do with being scared. At least, not of ghosts or anything like that. But," and Audrey lowered her voice, seeming both embarrassed and sad, "I guess I'm a little scared of Frank. I don't like the way he's starting to act. It's like he thinks scaring you is the most important thing in the world."

"Yeah."

Audrey took a deep breath. She pulled a pack of gum out of her pocket and took out a piece. She offered a piece to Hilary, who hesitated. "Don't worry," Audrey said.

"There aren't any spiders or worms in the gum. It's just normal, regular gum."

Hilary took the piece and thanked her.

"So, after I talk with you, I'm going to see Frank and tell him the same thing. I'm out. If he ever wants to go back to just scaring kids every once in a while, I'm in. But this Cemetery Club, it's getting too intense for me. I have no idea how that spider thing happened, and I don't really want to. But like I said, he's starting to worry me."

"Okay," said Hilary. She believed Audrey. The girl wasn't planning any scares for her as she stood outside the apartment door. "Thanks for telling me."

"I gotta go," said Audrey. "Just watch out for Frank. I'm not sure how far he'll take it."

Hilary nodded. Audrey turned and walked down the steps. Hilary shut the door.

Chapter 26

Frank slammed his front door. He couldn't believe it. Audrey was quitting the club! She said she came over because she thought it would be easier to explain in person, but Frank was so mad that he wouldn't even let her into his apartment.

How dare she do that to me? To Todd? We're a team!

Frank sat, hard, on one of the living room chairs. His mother, in the kitchen, called, "Who was that?"

"Nobody," Frank called back.

I can't believe it! She quit! Well, fine! Todd and I will be the club, just the two of us! Hilary isn't going to get the best of us!

Frank's phone rang. Frank reached into his pocket, pulled out his phone, and pressed "TALK."

"Yeah?"

"Frank, this is Hilary Wilson."

"It is?" he said then felt stupid. That was a dumb thing to say. "How'd you get my number?"

"From your mom. I called her a few minutes ago to talk to you, and she said I should call you directly."

Thanks for nothing, Mom! "So? What do you want?"

"Yeah," said Hilary. "I'm not coming to the club

meeting tonight. My family is going out to eat."

"Oh, yeah?"

"My whole family is going out. I don't have a choice."

"Sure you do. And you choose not to come to the club meeting."

"What are you trying to say, Frank?"

Frank looked around to make sure his mother wasn't within hearing distance. Then he said, "That you are admitting you're too scared. You're admitting I win."

"Win what, Frank?"

"I win, that's all. I win for being the bravest! You lose for being a wussy baby! You quit because you are too scared of what might happen next. So you see? I win!"

"You don't win! I'm not quitting. I just can't come tonight."

"Whatever," said Frank. "In fact, don't ever come to a Cemetery Club meeting again for all I care. But don't be surprised if scary things keep happening. Remember what we said, once a ghost is called up, you can't always send it back!"

"Frank, you are so…"

Frank pushed the red "END" button and shoved the phone back into his pocket.

No Audrey. And now, no Hilary. Fine, the Cemetery Club was canceled. It was dead. He would text Todd and tell him so. Todd hadn't been much help, anyway. He just liked to complain.

But Frank was determined to come up with new ways to keep Hilary scared. He wanted her to admit she was nothing more than a scaredy cat who should never have made fun of him in the first place.

And he would do what it took for that to happen.

It didn't matter that there was no more Cemetery Club. It was now going to be one-on-one. Just Frank and Hilary.

That'll be better! And I'm going to win.

He grinned and leaned back against the chair cushion.

Oh, yeah! I'm going to win!

Chapter 27

The day was cool and clear. In physical education class, the seventh graders had run the track, preparing for a physical fitness test. Hilary enjoyed it; it felt good to be out in the fresh air with the sun shining down. Audrey, who was in class with Hilary, wound up pacing herself with Hilary as they jogged along the track. They didn't talk much; Audrey only said, "Hey, Hilary," but it made Hilary think that since the Cemetery Club was over, Audrey might really want to be friends with her.

There was a social studies test, and Hilary, for the first time since she'd moved, felt she had really done well. She bet she'd have an "A" when she got her paper back. In math, she got all her homework done before class was over.

It was turning out to be a pretty good day.

After English class, she followed the flow of other students to the cafeteria. She sat at the end of a table by herself, watching to see if Audrey might join her. When Audrey came out from the kitchen with her tray, Hilary raised her hand to catch the girl's attention, but then she saw Frank waving to Audrey. Audrey glanced at Hilary, glanced at Frank, and then went over to sit with Frank.

Hilary lowered her hand. She felt silly and embarrassed and hurt. She opened her backpack to get out the apple she'd packed that morning. Without looking, she reached inside the bag.

Her fingers came down on something sticky and unfamiliar.

She jerked her hand back out. Slowly, she lifted the pack, put it on the table, and pulled it open father to look inside.

At first she wasn't sure what she was seeing. But then she knew.

Bones!

Hilary gasped, then looked around to see if anyone had heard her. No one had. They were busy eating, talking, and laughing with their friends. Even Frank and Audrey seemed busy with their own conversation.

Slowly, her hands shaking and her heart pounding, Hilary reached into the backpack. She picked up one of the bones and lifted it enough to see without taking it out. It was not one bone, but many small bones, tied together with string. They clacked back and forth like a nightmarish wind chime. They were covered with the sticky, reddish-brown substance.

Bloody bones!!

There was a note in the backpack beneath the bones, printed in red letters and surrounded in with a bluish glow.

"We, the ghosts of Resurrection Cemetery, are angry! And you can't send ghosts back once you call on them! These bones are a warning that we are after you! Ha ha ha ha ha!"

Chapter 28

Sitting next to Todd at the back of the school bus heading home, Frank watched Hilary at the front. He kept hoping she'd turn around and say something, to accuse him of putting the chicken bones into her backpack. He wanted to hear her say, "I give up! You win, Frank!" But she hadn't said a word. She acted like nothing had happened.

"Maybe she thinks a ghost really did put the bones in her backpack," Todd whispered.

Frank shook his head. He didn't think so. If she did, she would have made a scene in the cafeteria. She would have thrown her backpack away, or run out of the room, or started to cry.

But she didn't.

She didn't say or do anything that made him think she'd been frightened. Instead, she just put her backpack down and started eating her lunch.

So it was clear she knew he had put the bones in her pack. Now she was mad, even if she wasn't showing it.

This meant she was planning something in retaliation.

He knew the bone thing was kind of lame, but it was the best thing he could think of at the moment. He wanted to scare her right away, so she wouldn't have time to make the first move. And so he'd sneaked a package of chicken from the refrigerator last night and scraped most of the meat off the bones. He'd tied them together with dental floss, creating three clicky, clacky strands, and then put them into a plastic baggie to take to school the next day. Next, he'd used a red marker and some of the leftover glow-in-the-dark paint to make a note on an index card. The note warned Hilary that the ghosts of Resurrection Cemetery were angry.

In art class, while the teacher was helping other students with their pottery projects, he painted the bones with slow-drying oil paint, red with a little brown mixed in. *This will look and feel like blood,* he'd thought. *She'll freak out for sure!*

He wasn't sure how he would get the bones to Hilary without her seeing or knowing. The best place would have been in her locker, but of course, lockers had locks. He'd thought it would be cool to stick them in her coat pocket somehow while riding the bus to school in the morning, but she would have suspected something the moment he tried to move too close to her. Then the chance presented itself during English class; Hilary had gone to the restroom, and so Frank accidentally-on-purpose flung his pen down so it would roll away. When he crawled over to retrieve the pen, he pulled the bones from the baggie in his pocket and stuck them into Hilary's unzipped backpack along with the note. Todd and Audrey had watched him but didn't say a word. Audrey only shook her head disapprovingly. Frank had hoped Hilary would find the bones when she got back to the classroom. He wanted to see how well she hid her fear from everyone else in the classroom. But she didn't look in the pack until lunchtime.

And when she did, sitting there alone at the far table, she'd said nothing. She had looked around anxiously, but then zipped the pack closed and that was that. She didn't yell. She didn't come up to accuse him. She didn't tell anybody what she'd found.

And she still doesn't look scared enough, he thought as he watched the back of her head. *I want to see her scared, really scared!*

Tomorrow he'd have another little trick for Hilary. If the bones didn't do it, he knew he could come up with something that would.

He let out an angry breath, ignored Todd's rambling discussion about some movie he'd seen on television the other night, and turned to stare out the bus window.

Chapter 29

Hilary told Doreen she was going one block to the convenience store for some notebook paper. Doreen said, "Well, okay, but be back soon."

"Okay," Hilary replied. "Fifteen minutes, top."

She had plenty of notebook paper, and the store wasn't her destination. She headed, instead, across the street to Resurrection Cemetery.

Hurrying through the gate, she jogged along the twisting roads to the tree where she'd first seen the strange girl. She knew Marjorie could be anywhere today. Since Marjorie was probably homeless, she must sleep in the cemetery. Very sad, but likely. Today, if Hilary could find the girl, she would first take her home to her apartment and give her something to eat and something warm to wear. Then, quietly and privately in Hilary's room, she would ask Marjorie to come up with some new magic tricks that would show Frank once and for all that he would scare more quickly than she would. Those icky bones were the last straw.

"Marjorie?" she called from the base of the tree. Starlings, which had been settled on the lower branches, took off in a flutter of black wings. Hilary turned around, looking in all directions. "Marjorie, are you here? I need to talk with you!"

There was the sound of traffic outside the cemetery, the sound of crows calling to each other as they strutted around among tombstones, and the soft, whooshing sound of dead leaves falling to the grass around her feet. But there was no answer from Marjorie.

"Marjorie!" called Hilary. She had to find the girl before it got dark. "Marjorie, it's Hilary!"

Nothing.

"I need to talk to you!"

Nothing.

"Please? Marjorie! Can you hear me?"

And then Marjorie's voice, from above. "Well, hello, there!"

Hilary looked up. On a branch that Hilary could swear was empty a moment ago, Marjorie sat in her white dress and black shoes, swinging her legs in the air.

"Hi," said Hilary. "I thought you didn't like to climb trees."

"I said that? I don't remember. So, what's up?"

"You are," said Hilary.

Marjorie giggled lightly then climbed down from the tree. She stood in front of Hilary with her hands on her hips. Hilary thought, *She must be so cold in that dress!*

Hilary said, "You're my friend, right?"

Marjorie smiled and said, "Oh, certainly."

"I need your help."

"Of course," said Marjorie. "I'd love to help you. Let's sit down and talk about it." She gestured toward the grass beneath the tree.

"Well, I thought maybe we could go back to my apartment first. It's really warm inside. We could have a snack first, then talk. What do you think?"

Marjorie's eyebrows went up, then down. Then she said, "I can't really do that."

"Why not? It's not far."

"I just can't."

"But listen, okay? I have a book back in my bedroom. It's all about ghosts and other spooky things in this area. Frank knows a lot about all that. We could read it and come up with some things that would really make him scared!"

"I can't, Hilary."

Hilary sighed. It didn't make sense, but she said, "Okay."

"Let's sit, then," said Marjorie. "We can talk here."

The girls sat down in the grass. The dampness of the ground came up through the seat of Hilary's jeans quickly. She said, "Do you want to sit on my coat? It's pretty cold on the ground."

"No thanks," said Marjorie. "I'm just fine."

"Okay," said Hilary, marveling that Marjorie didn't care if she was cold or wet. "I want to tell you about the Cemetery Club. I know you sort of know what's going on, but there's more to it than that. It seems like the leader, Frank, has decided to do anything to scare me. Today, he put chicken bones in my backpack. And at first I thought they were bloody but then figured out it was sticky red paint. He also wrote a note saying that ghosts from this cemetery did it. It did scare me for a minute. But really, how stupid is he? He thinks stuff like that will make me believe those ghosts are real."

"What ghosts are those?" asked Marjorie.

"The ghosts of Karla and Marcus Beehan and some guy named Robert Richardson. Dumb, huh?"

"Yes, dumb," said Marjorie. "Karla, Marcus, and Robert are not ghosts."

"Of course not."

Marjorie nodded. "If he wanted real ghosts, he should have gone to some of the other gravesites."

Hilary frowned a little. "What?"

"You say he knows about the ghosts of this area? It doesn't seem like he knows very much at all. He doesn't know who is a ghost and who isn't."

"You mean...you believe in ghosts, Marjorie?"

Marjorie tilted her head. "Of course. Don't you?"

"No...not really."

Marjorie shrugged. "Oh. All right. So what you want is for me to scare Frank, right?"

"Yes," said Hilary. "Scare him enough so he leaves me alone. Really, really scare him. You seem to be great with tricks, like the recording and the worms and the spiders. You know, could make a living doing magic, I bet! Go on tour! Go to Las Vegas or Atlantic City!"

"Really?"

"But anyway, as to Frank, I don't want him to get hurt. I don't want anybody to get hurt. But I want him to tell me finally, 'I give up!' I want him to say, 'You win, Hilary!'"

"Okay," said Marjorie. "I'll help you."

"Great! Thanks! You know, I wish I knew how you did your tricks. Then I could help you!"

Marjorie shook her head.

"Yeah," said Hilary. "I figured you'd want to keep that to yourself. Anyway, about Frank. He lives in apartment number one in the middle building of our complex across Archer Road. We both go to Newberry Middle School. We're in the seventh grade. You know what he looks like."

"Yes."

"I don't think he'll be coming back to the cemetery now that his club's officially over, though. But still, since you know where he lives maybe you can think of something to do?"

Marjorie brought her knees up to her chin. Her white dress draped across her legs and hid her black shoes. She smiled, her blue eyes sparkling. "This will be fun."

Hilary stood, brushed off the seat of her jeans, and said, "I know you don't want to tell me how to do the tricks, but do you need any help? Anything I can do?"

"Oh, no," said Marjorie, still sitting in the grass. "I have to do this on my own. And I'll do a good job, I promise. I'll scare the boy. And I'll do it because we're friends. You said we were friends, didn't you?"

"Sure, we're friends," said Hilary, wondering if Marjorie had no other friends at all. They were so much alike that way. They only had each other.

"All right, then" said Marjorie. She held out her hand and Hilary leaned over to shake it. It was ice cold to the touch.

Poor girl! thought Hilary. *I really should bring her some warm clothes next time!*

"Just wait and see what I do to that boy!" said Marjorie.

"Great!" said Hilary. "Let's meet here tomorrow afternoon, okay?"

"Okay."

Hilary headed off down the road. Marjorie called after her, "Nothing will stop me, Hilary!"

Chapter 30

"Your mom called while you were out," said Doreen when Hilary came back into the apartment. "She says she had the tests at the hospital this morning and she's almost positive the results will be good. They'll know in a few days. She wanted you to know."

"Oh, that's great," said Hilary. She stopped and gave Doreen a genuine smile, for that was truly good news.

"Your mom's a wonderful person, you know," said Doreen.

"I know that," said Hilary.

"She has even told me she thinks you're doing okay, and that she won't need me for much longer."

"That's good."

"I'll miss you."

"Really? I've been kind of a brat." It was weird to admit it, but it was true.

Doreen laughed. "Hey, do you want to watch television with me? There's a really funny movie on."

"No, thanks.

"Or we could do some cooking. Make something extra special for your family's dinner tonight."

"I've got a lot homework to do." Hilary walked to the hallway.

Then Doreen said, "Hey, wait. I thought you went to get notebook paper at the store. Did you lose it along the way home?"

Hilary looked back at Doreen. "Um. Uh. They didn't have any. They were sold out. But that's okay. I have a few extra loose sheets in my backpack. I'll get some paper at the school store tomorrow."

"I could drive you to another store if you really need it. I don't mind."

"That's okay." Hilary went to her bedroom and closed the door. She plopped down on her bed and pulled the ghost book she'd bought at the bookstore from a drawer in the nightstand. She'd only had time to read the first two chapters. Now, though, she was going to read more, to find something to scare Frank. Maybe Marjorie didn't want any help with her trick, but it wouldn't hurt to have an idea of what to do. Tomorrow, she'd share her ideas with Marjorie.

"This will be great, I know it!" Hilary said to herself.

The book's table of contents listed Chicago-area ghosts and haunted places. She'd read a chapter on ghosts in Holy Sepulchre Cemetery and one chapter about a ghost light seen in Bachelor Grove Cemetery. There was even a chapter on the Hull House Devil Baby and one on ghosts of men who died when their ships sank in Lake Michigan.

She flipped past the section about the ghostly handprint of the firefighter, remembering it from Frank, Audrey, and Todd's dumb report in English class.

And then she stopped at the chapter about Resurrection

Cemetery and the ghost called Resurrection Mary.

"Resurrection Cemetery," Hilary said. "Yes! This should be perfect! Let's see what it says."

She flipped pages and began reading.

As she read, her eyes grew wider and wider.

"No one knows Resurrection Mary's real name," the book explained. "She died in an automobile accident in 1934. She has been appearing in and beside Resurrection Cemetery since 1939. She is a beautiful, young ghost who wears a white ball gown, the same one she was wearing when she was killed. She wears the same black dancing shoes, as well."

Hilary took a sharp breath, and continued reading.

"Mary sometimes appears on the side of Archer Road, asking for rides from strangers."

Marjorie wears a white dress all the time!

Marjorie wears black shoes!

I saw Marjorie hitching a ride on Archer Road!

Hilary put the book down in front of her. She stared at it, almost afraid to read any more. She remembered Audrey in English class, talking about this ghost. This was crazy. There was no way this could be true.

Impossible!

Hilary slapped the book from the bed. It fell to the floor, pages flapping like the wings of an injured bird. "There's no way Marjorie is a ghost. No way she is Resurrection Mary!"

But a ghost could perform magic tricks. A ghost could make people see things that weren't there, trick them, terrify them!

"Marjorie," said Hilary, as she stared at the book on the floor. "Could you really be a ghost?"

Chapter 31

"Ms. Bruce," said Hilary after English class was over. "I was wondering if you still had the reports the kids gave last week."

Ms. Bruce looked up from her desk. "The oral reports?"

"Yep."

"I've graded most of them, Hilary. I still have a few to do. But, wait. You didn't have to do one. Why do you ask?"

"I was wondering about the resource page from Frank, Audrey, and Todd's report. I know they had to turn in a bibliography. If you haven't graded the report and given it back, I was wondering if I could see that one page."

"You want to know what resources they used?"

Hilary nodded. "I just want to find a book they might have used. I want to read it."

Ms. Bruce touched her chin with her index finger. "Why don't you just ask them?"

Hilary hesitated. "I guess I could, but, well, I thought if you had the paper, I could just look at that."

Ms. Bruce pulled a small stack of papers from the right side of her desk and thumbed through them. She took out a report. "Here is theirs," she said. "You just want to see the bibliography?"

Hilary nodded. Ms. Bruce turned to the last sheet. "I can't take this off for you. You'll have to look at it here."

"That's okay," said Hilary. She quickly read over the list of books the three had used in preparing their report. Then she said, "Thanks."

"You're welcome, Hilary." As Hilary turned to leave, Ms. Bruce said, "I hope you are starting to feel at home here at our school. I know it's hard to be the new kid."

"I'm doing okay," said Hilary. "Thanks."

Social studies class followed lunch. During the period, students were sent to the school library to research their favorite president. Hilary, with a list of books she'd scribbled down from memory, went looking for ghost books.

Frank's science class was in the library at the same time, and when she saw him, she cringed. Still, she made a point not to show any emotion. Not fear, not anger, not anything. Let him wonder what she was thinking. Let him wonder what she might be planning next, if anything. As so, as she glanced over at him and he glanced up at her, she did her best to look aloof and unaffected before she turned away.

Hilary rummaged through the library shelves, looking for the ghost books. She found all three of those on her list from the Cemetery Club's report. Then, she sat in a corner study carrel and began to read.

The first book was worthless, only dealing with ghosts in general, not those around Chicago. Hilary put that book aside. The second dealt with ghostly actions and behaviors. One line read, "Although some ghosts can actually cause harm to humans, such as the Bell Witch of Tennessee who hit and slapped several unfortunate people, causing them to fall down or their faces to bruise, most ghosts can only create illusions. Illusions that can be seen, heard, smelled, and sometimes felt. While these illusions appear real, they don't last long and create no actual danger."

Hilary ran her finger down the page and read another line: "While many ghosts are confined to the area in which they died or were buried, some are able to travel a several-mile radius from these places."

And then at the top of the next page, she read, "When ghosts are called upon, they are known to get out of control. It is believed that once a ghost is called for, it cannot be sent back."

Wow, thought Hilary. *That is what Frank said. But I just can't believe it!*

Hilary closed that book and picked up third. It had a chapter of famous ghosts of the Midwest. There was a small section on Resurrection Mary. "She often hitches a ride along Archer Road near the cemetery but then vanishes from the passenger's seat as if she were never there, leaving the driver shaken and confused. Other times she has hitched rides from the far end of the cemetery and asks to be let out at the main gate. As she walks into the cemetery, she disappears into thin air. Mary still wears the white gown and black shoes she wore the night she died in the car wreck. On occasion, she has been seen inside the cemetery. No one knows her actual identity, though there have been some speculations."

Hilary looked around to make sure Frank hadn't come over, looking for her. He hadn't. She was still alone in the corner carrel.

She continued reading: "Resurrection Mary's skin, according to those few who have touched her, is quite cold, as if from the tomb, as if from a grave."

I touched Marjorie, Hilary thought. *And her skin really is cold. But...but she doesn't wear a coat or scarf or gloves. Anybody would have cold hands in October without gloves on!*

Hilary got up and took the books back to the shelf. She took a long breath and put her hands on her hips.

Marjorie can't be Resurrection Mary. There are no such things as ghosts.

I have to stop letting my imagination run away with me!

There was a sudden, loud rumbling behind her. Hilary whipped about to see a whole row of books bouncing up and down on one of the shelves. The books shivered and shook and hopped, as if an earthquake was underneath them. Yet the books on other shelves were not moving at all. Hilary gasped and stumbled backward.

"Hey, what's happening?" shouted someone nearby.

Everyone at the nearby tables had stopped what they were doing. They all stared at the books dancing on the shelf.

Then, one by one, the books blew off the shelf, covers wobbling and pages fluttering, hurtling through the air as if someone with the strength of ten people had pushed them from behind. Kids screamed as the books flew across the room in line straight toward Frank, who still sat on a cushioned bench. His face fell open with an expression of sheer terror. He cried out and dove to the carpet. The books kept going, flying over his head, until they hit the far wall and dropped to the floor.

Slam slam slam slam slam slam slam!

"What in the world is going on?" shouted the librarian, who had been in her office. She had come out when she heard the kids break into loud talking. She had not seen the books flying.

Most of the kids turned to her and began at once to tell her what they'd seen. It was a jumble. The librarian couldn't understand them and kept putting her finger to her mouth to quiet them. Then, at last, they stopped talking and the librarian said, "All right. One person tell me. What's going on?"

"Books!" said a short, skinny boy with dark hair. "They flew right off the bookshelf! They flew over there like they wanted to hit Frank and..."

"Hey!" said a tall, red-haired girl. "They're gone!"

All the kids looked at the wall where the books had stuck and fallen. There were no books there at all. In fact, all the books that had shot across the library were back on the shelf as if they've never been gone at all.

Frank, however, was still on the floor, lying flat with his hands over his head.

"Wow!" said the short boy. "How'd that happen?"

"Yeah," said a girl in Hilary's social studies class, a girl whose name she didn't know. "We all saw those books go flying!"

The librarian went over to Frank. "Are you all right, Frank? Are you hurt?"

At last, Frank rolled over and slowly got to his feet. His expression of terror had changed to one of sheer rage. "I'm fine," he managed to say. The librarian looked at him for a moment, then told the kids to settle down. She returned to her office.

"That was wild!" said one boy. And then all the kids started talking, laughing nervously, huddling together.

"That was really scary!"

"It was really cool!"

"How did it happen?"

"I don't know!"

None of them paid any attention to Hilary.

Except for Frank.

He took several steps forward, pointed a finger at Hilary, and said in a whisper, "You! You aren't getting away with your tricks. You can't scare me, no matter what! No matter *what*!" Then he turned and stormed out of the library.

Oh, my gosh! thought Hilary. *It was Marjorie! She told me how she can make people imagine things!*

Hilary looked at the chattering students, then over at the shelf where the books sat motionless just like books should. Her own body trembled madly.

Marjorie is a ghost! I've asked her for help in scaring Frank and she was really excited about helping! Oh, no! What have I done?

What have I done?

Chapter 32

Hilary was afraid to get on the bus with Frank after school. She didn't know what he might try to do to get back at her for the attack of the books. Even though she'd had nothing to do with the books! Audrey had warned Hilary to stay away from him. Yet Hilary had not been able to let it go. She had so been determined to win the contest of who was bravest.

And now, Marjorie was involved.

What a mistake it was to have gotten her involved!

Hilary climbed onto the bus and found a seat directly behind the driver. Frank was far in the back with Todd, which was good. Audrey was in the middle, gazing out the window. Hilary tried to get Audrey's attention; she hoped the girl might move up front and sit with her. That way, Hilary would explain what was going on. It would be nice to have someone on Hilary's side. But Audrey wouldn't look around. She just stared out the window.

When I get home I've got to find Marjorie, Hilary thought as she turned back around to face out the front windshield of the bus. *I've got to tell her not to help me anymore!*

The bus drove along as usual, and for the first few

minutes everything seemed calm. Nervous, Hilary tried to catch a glimpse of Frank in the driver's rearview mirror, but he was just out of view.

That's good, really. I don't want to see him. I just want to make sure he's not trying to sneak up on me.

Hilary pulled her backpack into her stomach.

I didn't mean to cause any real trouble. I didn't mean to invite a ghost to help me. I didn't even believe in ghosts until this afternoon!

Hilary's lungs hurt from worry. She shut her eyes and put her face on the backpack.

And then there was a screech and then screams from the back of the bus. Hilary spun around to look down the aisle. She couldn't hear Frank's shouts over the sudden, terrified squeals of the other students.

There were bats, big and furry and brown with huge, glistening fangs, circling around Frank's head. He slapped at them, his mouth stretched and teeth bared in horror. Todd scrambled up and over to the seat in front of him, and ducked down with his arms covering his head.

But the bats weren't after Todd. They were after Frank.

"Help me!" cried Frank.

The other kids were on their feet, jumping up and down, yelling, and pointing at the bats. The bats buzzed like huge insects, darting about to slap Frank on the head with their leathery wings.

"Help me!" Frank cried. He smacked at the bats and the bats smacked him back.

"Mr. Lawson!" shouted the other students. "Mr. Lawson!"

The bus pulled to the side of the road in one quick,

jerky motion. Hilary's backpack slid from her lap to the sticky bus floor. Mr. Lawson, the bus driver, slammed the gearshift into "park," stood up, and spun around, shouting, "Who's back there fighting? Stop that this minute!"

Hilary looked back at Frank. He had gotten to his feet in the aisle but was still screaming. His hair was tangled and his face was flushed.

But the bats were gone.

"We saw bats!" the students shouted to the bus driver.

Mr. Lawson just said, "Do you guys know you could have caused a wreck with all that commotion?"

"No, listen, Mr. Lawson! We saw bats! Big ones!"

Mr. Lawson held up his hand. "Enough of that. Now you guys be quiet so we can get you home. You understand?"

A number of kids said, "But we really did see bats! They were after Frank!"

"Be quiet and sit down in your seats!"

"But we saw them!" the students insisted. "Then they disappeared!"

"Enough of your wild imaginations! Now either get quiet and stay seated, or I'll just call all of your parents and tell them they can come pick you up right here by the road. I'm sure they would be very unhappy about that."

Hilary could hear the urgent grumblings among the students:

"He doesn't believe us. But it's true!"

"You saw it right?"

"Yeah, I sure did!"

"Frank, why did they attack you?"

"Yeah, Frank, what's up with that?"

Frank, who was back in his seat, just said, "Shut up."

It was then that Hilary noticed Audrey staring at her as if Hilary were a ghost. Audrey's eyes were huge and her forehead furrowed. Slowly, she mouthed, "What did you just do?"

Hilary mouthed back, "I didn't do anything! It wasn't me!"

But it was clear Audrey didn't believe her. She just shivered and turned away.

Hilary stared at the floor of the bus, where her backpack lay. *This could go on and on, getting worse and worse! I don't want to think about how bad it might get!*

There was no doubt that Frank was frightened. He would either admit it or do what he could to make it worse for Hilary. Then Marjorie would do something, and then Frank, and then Marjorie, and then Frank and on and on and on.

When the bus pulled up in front of the apartment complex, Hilary rushed off and into the building before Frank could get to the bus door. She didn't want to see him. She didn't want to be anywhere near him. Her legs felt wobbly and her teeth chattered.

Maybe I can be sick from school the rest of the week, she thought as she slipped her key into her apartment door. *Or maybe the game store will fail and we can move back to Pennsylvania! I don't want to live here! I hate it here!*

Doreen wasn't watching television or reading in the living room like she usually was. Maybe she was in the bathroom. Hilary threw her backpack onto the sofa and went into the kitchen for something to drink. Her throat was sore and dry, and her nerves continued to jangle. She found a pitcher of limeade and poured a glass. Her hands shook so bad she was surprised she didn't drop the whole thing.

"Hilary?" It was her mother's voice.

"Mom?" Hilary took her glass of limeade into the hall.

"I'm in here, honey."

Mrs. Wilson was in her bedroom, propped up on her bed against a couple of pillows, reading a magazine. "Hi, Sweetie," she said with a gentle smile. Her voice was very tired.

"Hey, whatcha doing home?" asked Hilary. "Where's Doreen?"

"I told her she could go on home. I left the store early. I don't feel very well."

"You aren't really sick again, are you?"

"I don't know, Hilary. I hope not."

Hilary's heart clenched. The thought of all the lying and sneaking she'd been doing over the past many days twisted in her chest like shards of glass. She went into the room and sat gently on the side of the bed. "Is there anything I can do, Mom?"

Mrs. Wilson shook her head and then took Hilary's hand. "Just stay here with me, honey. That's all. Douglas doesn't have late practice today, so he'll be home in just an hour or so. If you could just stay around in case I need you."

I have to find Marjorie right away! Hilary thought. *I bet she's planning more things to do, things that could cause some really bad trouble! I have to tell her I don't want her help anymore!*

Then Hilary stopped. She looked at her mother, who

was pale and frail but still smiling, and thought, *But my mom needs me! I love her so much and I don't want her to be sick!*

Hilary began to cry, painful, heaving sobs that felt as if they would burst right through her chest. Things with Frank and Marjorie had gotten so messed up, so tangled up and scary, but the idea of her mother getting so sick again was scarier and sadder than anything else.

"Honey, what's wrong?" asked her mother with a gentle squeeze of Hilary's hand.

"Everything!"

"Do you want to talk about it?"

"I…I don't…" She could say no more. *How can I tell her what's going on? I'm scared and sad and everything is so messed up!*

Mrs. Wilson nodded. "Hilary, things will get better. Each day is the chance for something to change in a positive direction. Don't forget that. And don't forget that we are strong people. I'm strong. Your dad and Douglas are strong. And so are you."

"I'm not strong at all."

"Don't say that. You're talking about my daughter, after all. She's smart, brave, caring, and kind."

"But I'm not! I'm stupid, a coward, and selfish!"

Mrs. Wilson drew Hilary down into a warm and comforting embrace. She whispered into Hilary's hair, "I love you, and you are all those good things I said. Maybe you don't feel it right now, but it's true."

As they hugged, Hilary's sobs eased. They held each other for several minutes. Then Hilary sat up and wiped her eyes. "Thanks, Mom," she said, her voice still trembling.

"Anytime, honey."

"Now why don't you take a nap? I'll be here. Just let me know if you need anything. Something to eat or drink? I could rub your back."

Mrs. Wilson smiled. "I'll let you know, honey."

"Want me to turn off the light?"

"Sure. That would be good."

Hilary walked to the door, flicked off the light, and then watched as her mother slipped down beneath the covers. Hilary pulled the door closed and walked back down the hall.

"Maybe I've been stupid and cowardly," she said to herself as she sat on the sofa in the living room. "But not anymore. I'm going to set things right!"

She picked up the phone receiver, and as she dialed Frank's apartment, she thought, *I'll tell him exactly what's going on. I'll tell him I didn't mean it to get so bad, so dangerous. I'll even admit he won, that he's the king of the Cemetery Club! I don't care anymore. It's not important at all!*

On the fourth ring, someone answered. The voice was deep and furious.

"Hello!"

"Is...is this Frank?" asked Hilary.

"Hilary, is that you?" Yes, it was Frank. And it sounded like he didn't want to hear anything she had to say.

"Yeah, it's me," she said. "I called because..."

"Because you wanted to know how I like the snakes you put in my bathtub!"

"What!?"

"Well, I hate them! Just like you hoped I would! I don't

know how you're making all this happen, but you just wait! You just wait, Hilary!"

"Snakes in your bathtub? Oh, no! Frank, I'm sorry!"

"They're gone now, just like the books and the bats, but I'm planning something that will scare you so bad you won't ever want to leave your apartment!"

"Frank, listen to me! It's not what I meant to happen. I didn't do it! It wasn't me. I just asked someone to help me scare you!"

"I'm not scared! I don't care what you do!"

"That someone was a ghost, Frank."

"A ghost? There's no such thing as ghosts!"

"I didn't think so, either!"

"You're crazy!"

"No, listen to me! I asked a ghost to help me but I didn't know she was a ghost! The ghosts you called up in the cemetery aren't real, but the one I met is real! She's making things appear, but they're just illusions. The rocks, the bats, the books, the snakes!"

"I'm not that stupid, Hilary!"

"I'm going to make her stop!"

"I said I'm not that stupid! You want me to be scared and then you want me to say I believe you so I'll look stupid! I'm not falling for that!"

"Frank!"

But he hung up. Hilary sat, holding the receiver. Slowly, she put it back into the cradle.

She had to go see Marjorie.

But she had to stay with her mother.

What am I going to do?!

Just then the door opened and Douglas came into the

apartment. Hilary grabbed him by the arm.

"I'm so glad you're home!"

Douglas tilted his head and chuckled. "Okay, Hilary, what do you need from me?"

"Just stay here with Mom while I run out for a few minutes."

Douglas' smile faltered. "Now what?"

"It's something I have to do. Trust me!"

"What things? Are you in trouble?"

"I…well, not really."

"Wait, what's going on, Hilary?"

"Just a few minutes! If you trust me this one time I promise I'll never lie or sneak again and I'll even stop fussing about Doreen and I'll clean your room for you for a week or do your laundry for a week or whatever you ask, okay? Please please please?"

"Hilary, wait."

"Thanks, Douglas!" said Hilary as she went out the door. "And don't worry! I'll be okay! I'll make it quick!"

With that, she rushed down the steps.

Chapter 33

She didn't take time to walk to the main gate. She stood outside the green iron fence, her face pressed between the bars, and shouted, "Marjorie! I know you're in there! And I know who you are now! Please come talk to me!"

Inside the cemetery, dying leaves swirled from tree branches, sweeping down and covering the grass. There didn't seem to be many visitors to the cemetery; those Hilary could see were far off in the distance. The air was damp and chilly.

"Marjorie! I know you can hear me!"

A breeze picked up, throwing dead leaves against the bottom of the iron fence. Several blew through the bars and caught on her shoe. She shook them off.

"Marjorie! You have to listen to me! I don't need your help anymore. It's more than I wanted! I didn't know things would be like this!"

There was no answer.

"Marjorie! Do you hear me! Don't help me anymore!"

Still, there was no answer.

"Marjorie! Where are you?"

Above her head, several starlings flew, wings fluttering, from one tree to another.

Hilary shook the bars. "Marjorie, I mean it! Answer me now!"

And then a voice whispered against Hilary's ear. A bodiless voice, coming through the fence like the wind.

"Hilary," the voice said. "You said you needed my help. Nobody's ever needed my help before. And you said we're friends."

Hilary looked all around, trying to see where Marjorie was. But only the voice was there. "We…we are friends," Hilary replied. "But you have to…"

"You wanted me to scare that boy like he's never been scared before. I'm doing that, for certain!" The voice chuckled darkly.

"Marjorie, listen to me!"

But it was as if Marjorie couldn't hear Hilary. It was as if she was talking to herself. "I may be trapped here, in and around the cemetery, but my power can reach farther. As far as the school, the bus, the apartment building! I'm having so much fun, scaring Frank."

"I don't want your help anymore!" shouted Hilary.

"So much fun. So much fun."

Hilary's took a deep, shuddering breath. She had a question to ask. She hoped Marjorie would hear her. "Marjorie," she said, "is that your real name? Or is it…is it Mary?"

"Mary?" came the whisper.

"Yes," said Hilary. "What is your real name?"

There was a pause, and then, "I don't remember my real name. It might be Mary. Marjorie. Martha. It's been so long. Too long to remember, so long since the accident."

Hilary licked her lips. They were as dry as the dead

leaves. Then she asked, “Are you a ghost?”

The whisper turned into a giggle. The giggle grew into laughter, loud laughter, rising up and around the fence, whirling around Hilary’s head. Hilary put her hands over her ears but the sound came through. Then, abruptly, the laughter stopped. The voice answered, “Of course I am! I thought you knew that.”

Hilary said, “Please!”

The voice began to fade. “I’m your friend.”

“Don’t scare Frank anymore. Stop it now! It’s too much. It’s over with!”

“I’m going to help you. I’m your friend, I’m your friend, I’m your friend.”

Then the voice was gone.

Hilary put her forehead against the fence. She stared at the ground, where leaves spun in tiny circles in the breeze. She kicked at them, hard.

They didn’t move away. They continued to spin, determined to do what they wanted, no matter what.

Just like Marjorie.

Chapter 34

Frank couldn't sit down. He walked back and forth across the rug in his living room, mumbling to himself, glancing over his shoulder every few moments to make sure nothing else was going to come flying at his head.

He was scared. Really scared. He never knew he could be so scared.

He had two choices. He could try to think of something to scare Hilary even worse, or he could just tell her he gave up.

But he didn't want to give up. What would Todd and Audrey say? They'd call him a chicken, a coward!

But what could he do to scare Hilary now? He thought the red-painted bones were scary, but clearly they were stupid! They were nothing compared to what Hilary was able to do. She seemed to know more about terrifying magic tricks than anyone he'd ever met. What could he do that was scarier than the books or the bats or the snakes?

Suddenly, the phone rang. Frank almost jumped out of his skin. It rang again. He reached over carefully and picked it up. What if something came crawling out of the receiver?

"Hello?"

"Frank." It was his mother. "I need you to put the casserole in the freezer into the oven at three seventy-five. I'm shopping and need to get some gas in the car before I come home."

Frank thought, *Mom, I wish you knew what was happening. But I can't tell you! You'd think I was crazy! Or you'd be so mad you'd ground me for a year!*

"Frank, did you hear me?"

"I heard you. I'll put it in."

"Okay, then. I'll see you soon." She hung up.

Frank threw the phone onto the coffee table and crossed his arms over his chest.

What can I do to get back at Hilary? How does she do all those things? Is she a witch or something? No, of course not. There are no such things as witches. Or ghosts.

The phone rang again. Frank jumped again, and he stared at the phone on the table. Now who was that?

He reached over. He hesitated. Maybe the phone was red hot now. Maybe it would turn into a scorpion when he picked it up.

Why do I like scaring people?

"I hate being scared!" he said aloud.

Cautiously, he touched the phone as it rang again. It felt all right. He picked it up and put it to his ear. In a raspy voice, he said, "Hello?"

"Is this Frank Smith?"

"Yes."

"This is Mrs. Wilson, Hilary's mom."

Uh-oh. Now what?

"I was wondering if she was down in your apartment.

I thought she was staying here with me but I just woke up and she is gone. Her brother said she rushed out in a hurry, and I thought maybe she'd gone down to see you."

"Hilary? No, she's not here."

"Doreen told me that sometimes she watches movies with you, so I thought maybe she…"

"She's not here. Sorry."

"Well," came Mrs. Wilson's voice. It was soft and weak, like she wasn't feeling very well. "Thanks anyway, Frank."

"No problem, Mrs. Wilson," said Frank. But what he saw coming from beneath the front door of his apartment made him drop the phone. It hit the floor and bounced.

"Oh no!" he cried.

Mrs. Wilson's voice could be heard from the phone, sounding very far away. "What is it, Frank? What's the matter?"

Frank stared at the thick, gray smoke pouring into his apartment from the hallway.

Finally, he found his voice.

"Fire!"

Chapter 35

Hilary's thoughts flew around like crazy insects as she hurried back across Archer Road. She couldn't stop Marjorie, so that meant Frank was going to be tricked more and more. And that meant he would want to trick her more and more. Someone was going to get hurt, she was sure of it.

How did I get in this mess in the first place? This is horrible! It's getting worse and worse! I've been so stupid!

She walked slowly, dragging her feet through the gravel of the parking lot. A car, pulling in behind her, honked its horn to get her to move out of the way. She stepped to the side.

"I should tell Douglas," she said to herself. "Maybe he can help me."

But how? He doesn't believe in anything supernatural, especially not ghosts!

Hilary looked down at her shoes then up at the sky. Her neck hurt with worry. Her eyes stung with fresh tears that wanted to come out.

She got to the sidewalk in front of her apartment building and stopped. She'd go inside, sit down for a little while, and rest. Then maybe she would tell her mother. It had been a long time since she'd really talked with her mom, and she missed doing it. Mom surely wouldn't believe the ghost part, and she would be angry at the times Hilary had lied, but she was a mom, and most of the time moms were really good listeners.

I hope she forgives me.

Hilary reached the sidewalk that led to her apartment building.

And suddenly the apartment's front door burst open and thick, dark smoke rolled out. Several people poured out of the building along with the smoke, their hands over their faces, their eyes huge and terrified.

"No!" Hilary screamed.

She ran toward the door. A man who had come out grabbed her arm and said, "Don't go in there! It's too dangerous!"

But Hilary knew it was Marjorie. She made the fire to scare Frank! It was only an illusion.

"Let me go!" she cried, jerking her arm away. She raced up the stoop and stopped, wanting to be sure before she rushed inside. The smoke was thick, and she could see flames through the open doorway. They were everywhere—bright orange and red flames on the stairs and licking the walls. She could hear the shouts of others who were still in the building.

But her eyes didn't sting from the smoke. And the fire wasn't hot. She was right. It was one of Marjorie's terrible illusions.

"I knew it! It's not real!" she cried, hoping the people would hear her and believe her. "Don't panic!"

Hilary raced into the building to Frank's apartment

door. She pounded on it with her fists. "Frank, come out! It's not real, don't worry!"

"I can't! I don't want to burn up!" came Frank's voice from inside. "Go away!"

"Frank, please! I promise, it's not real! Come out!"

"Hilary, I admit it, okay? I'm scared! So will you stop this? Stop this, please! I can't stand it anymore!"

"I admit it, too, Frank! I'm scared, too! We're both scared! We're both brave but we both can get scared! Now please come out! I promise, the fire isn't real! I want to prove it to you!"

The door opened a crack. Frank, his eyes squinted up in the smoke, peeked out. Hilary pushed the door open and took him by the hand. She led him outside to the grass where more people had gathered.

"Just stay here until it disappears," Hilary told Frank. "It won't last. Believe me, okay? It won't last, and it won't hurt anyone."

"You're doing it!"

"No, it's not me," said Hilary. "It's Marjorie! The ghost! And the fire isn't real!"

"What is she talking about?" said one older man.

"It's an imaginary fire," said Hilary. "I know it sounds totally weird but..."

Then a horrified cry came from inside the building, from the stairway. "Hilary! Where are you?"

Hilary spun around. Her blood ran cold with fear. "Mom!"

She ran back into the building, trying to see through the smoke and fire. There, halfway down the bottom flight of stairs stood her mother, wearing her nightgown, holding on to the bannister. Douglas was at the top of the stairs, hurrying down after her.

"Mom, be careful!" Hilary shouted.

"Hilary, get out get out!" cried her mother. And she let go of the bannister and reached one arm out to point the way to the door. She lost her balance, fell forward, and tumbled down the steps.

"Mom!" cried Hilary.

"Mom!" shouted Douglas.

Mrs. Wilson hit the floor at the bottom of the stairs. She groaned once and then was silent.

"Mom!" Hilary dropped beside her mother. "Mom, no! Please, Mom, be okay!"

Her mother didn't speak. She didn't move.

Douglas jumped down beside them, his face twisted in anguish, and he quickly dialed 911 on his cell phone.

As Hilary held her mother's hand and wept, she didn't notice that the fire had finally disappeared, and all the smoke had vanished.

Chapter 36

Hilary sat on the front steps outside her apartment building, her head in her hands. Her father said she didn't have to go to school today. He knew how upset she was. Mrs. Wilson was in the hospital, her shoulder dislocated and her spleen ruptured in the fall. The doctors had assured the family that she would heal, but it would take longer because she wasn't physically a very strong woman.

"It wouldn't have happened if it wasn't for me," Hilary said to herself. "It's all my fault."

She took a deep breath and closed her eyes. Tears welled up and fell down her cheeks.

"Hey," came a voice from beside her. She looked up. Audrey stood there, wearing her red coat and a sad expression. "I heard about your Mom. I'm sorry she got hurt."

"How did you know?" asked Hilary.

"Frank called me last night. He told me about the fire that wasn't really a fire and about everyone running out but nothing getting burned. And he told me that your mom fell down the steps."

"Yeah," said Hilary.

Audrey sat on the step beside Hilary. "I guessed you wouldn't be at school today. So I skipped."

"You'll get in bad trouble."

Audrey shrugged. "Maybe not. I thought you might want someone to talk to or something."

Hilary shook her head. "I don't know what to say. You wouldn't believe me if I told you, anyway."

"Want to try?"

"Well," said Hilary. "Okay. But don't laugh."

"I won't."

Hilary told Audrey all about Marjorie, and how she found out that she was really Resurrection Mary, the ghost Audrey had told about in the class report. When Hilary was through, she looked at Audrey, expecting the girl to be giggling or at least smiling. Instead, Audrey looked concerned. She said, "Wow, a real ghost."

"Yeah."

"Let's go have a talk with that ghost and make her stop this nonsense."

"I tried!" said Hilary.

"Then let's try again."

"I'm scared, Audrey."

"Me, too. But if we go together we'll be less scared."

Audrey stood up. Hilary did, too. The two girls walked out of the parking lot, across Archer Road, and down to the entrance gate. As they went into the cemetery between the tall concrete pillars, Hilary felt the fingers of a cold breeze tickle her neck beneath her hair. She didn't want to face the ghost again, but Audrey was right. She had to try.

They walked for a few minutes in silence, down a roadway through the cemetery. Hilary spied the maple tree where Hilary had first met Marjorie.

Mary.

"Let's stop here," she said.

They stopped. Hilary put her hands on her hips. "Marjorie!" she called. "I have to talk to you!"

There was no answer.

"Marjorie!"

Still no answer.

Hilary turned to Audrey. "Maybe I have to be alone. Stay here. I won't go far."

"You sure?"

"I think so."

Hilary left the road and walked through the grass to the tree. She sat down beside the headstone of Patrick Oliver O'Toole, her legs crossed. If she lied, maybe Marjorie would come talk to her.

One more lie. The last one I'll ever tell, she promised herself.

"Marjorie! Come see me! I have a great new idea, a new trick for Frank! I want to talk to you about it!"

There was only silence.

"Okay? Marjorie?" called Hilary. *Ghosts can create illusions*, she thought, *but I don't think they can read minds!* "Do you hear me, Marjorie? It'll be fun!"

There was a rustling sound nearby, and Hilary turned to look beside her. Marjorie was there, sitting in the grass just a few feet away. She was in her white dress, black shoes, and yellow shawl. She smiled at Hilary. Hilary flinched at the smile. It was scary, knowing Marjorie's terrible power.

"Do you really have a new idea?" asked Marjorie. "Tell me about it!"

A chilling rush of fear coursed down Hilary's back. It was all she could do to keep from shaking. She was talking face to face with a ghost. An honest-to-goodness ghost. "Marjorie," she said. "You did good tricks. They really scared Frank. Scared a lot of other people, too."

"I know!" said Marjorie happily.

"But the new trick is this. No more tricks at all."

"I don't understand."

"Yes, you do," said Hilary. "You do understand. I don't want any more tricks. Frank and I both told each other we were scared. And so the contest is over. No more tricks."

Marjorie frowned. Her blue eyes turned red and her lip curled up over her teeth, which now looked sharp and terrifying. It was all Hilary could do to stay seated and not get up and run away.

"I don't want to stop!" said Marjorie. "You can't make me."

"Marjorie," Hilary managed, "you said we were friends. I'm asking you as a friend to stop the tricks. They're dangerous. People have been hurt!"

"I didn't hurt them!" said Marjorie.

"No, but your illusions did. And now, you have to go back wherever you came from. You can't play tricks anymore. I like you, but this has to stop."

Marjorie jumped up and pointed a finger at Hilary. "If you liked me you wouldn't ask me to go away!"

"I like you."

"No, you don't!"

"I do."

"You don't like me at all!" screamed Marjorie. "So how do you like this?"

Suddenly there was a roar behind Hilary. She clambered to her feet and spun around. There, standing in the grass, leaning toward her with its mouth open and fangs glistening, was a silver-scaled dragon. It roared again. The breath was as hot as an oven. It leaned in, its mouth ready to gulp Hilary in a single bite.

Hilary put her hands over her ears. "It's not real!" she shouted. The dragon waggled its huge head, pulled it back, and then disappeared, vanishing like a breath of frosty air. "Marjorie, no more illusions! Please!"

"How about this!" Marjorie cried.

The ground beneath Hilary's feet rumbled violently. The grass began to ripple and the soil began to bow as if it was a wave on the sea. Hilary stumbled backward, but she managed to stay on her feet. The ground suddenly split open beneath Patrick O'Toole's grave with a crunching and hissing, and a skeleton, cackling and laughing, leaped from the hole in the ground. The tombstone fell with a thud.

Hilary's throat closed; she could hardly take a breath. Her heart lurched and began to beat in double-time. *No! This is pretend! It's not real!*

The skeleton opened its rattly jaws and said, "Hilary, I'm going to take you with me to my home in the ground!" The bony fingers reached out, grasping for her.

Hilary found her breath and her voice. "No no no! It's an illusion! Stop it, Marjorie! I'm your friend, don't do this to me!"

The skeleton vanished.

Furious, terrified tears filled Hilary's eyes. She looked up at Marjorie, whose face was still taunting and mad. "Marjorie, please listen to me…"

"See how you like this one, then," Marjorie said, slowly. She pointed to Patrick O'Toole's tombstone, which was erect again. Mr. O'Toole's name was gone, and what was written there made Hilary's blood run cold.

"Patricia Elaine Wilson. Died October 31st of cancer. Rest In Peace."

"That's my, my mother!" cried Hilary.

"Yes, your mother," said Marjorie with an evil smile. "She's sick isn't she? What do you think of this, Hilary? Is it an illusion?"

"My mother!"

"Are you still my friend now, Hilary? I'm good at tricks, don't you think?"

Hilary raised her fists. "I hate you! I hate you, Marjorie! You're horrible! I'm not your friend at all!" She dropped to the ground on her knees. Her head fell forward and she began to cry. "I hate you, I hate you, I hate you!"

It seemed like hours before she could look back up again. It was when she felt a hand on her shoulder that she finally could. Through eyes that were swollen with tears, she saw Audrey standing there, looking down.

"Hilary, what happened?"

Hilary looked at the tombstone. Patrick Oliver O'Toole's name was there once more. The dreadful engraving with her mother's name was gone.

Marjorie was gone, too.

"What happened?" Audrey repeated as she helped Hilary to her feet. "Are you okay? Why are you crying?"

Hilary took deep breaths, trying to calm herself. She said, "I'm not sure yet."

Then she saw something at the base of the tombstone. There in the grass was a note and a single white rose. Hilary picked them up.

The note read, "*Dear Hilary. I know you liked me. I liked you, too. That was the problem. Ghosts aren't supposed to have friends in the real world. I had fun scaring Frank, but then you made me realize I had gone too far. Yet it was your friendship that kept me here. I couldn't tell you that while you were my friend. That is against the rules. And so I had to make you hate me. Only then could I go back to being a true ghost, one that comes out only now and then, one that doesn't do magic tricks for people. I'm sorry I had to upset you so much. But it was the only way for us to be free of each other.*"

"Oh," said Hilary. "That's so sad."

"What's sad?" asked Audrey. "What did you pick up?"

Hilary realized that Audrey couldn't see the note or the flower.

The note continued. "*Thank you for being my friend for a little while, though. It's something I'll always remember. Love, Mary.*"

Hilary said, "Maybe her name really was Mary."

"Whose name?" asked Audrey. "What are you talking about?"

Hilary smiled a little, and as she watched, both the note and the flower disappeared from her hands. They, too, were only illusions.

Hilary and Audrey walked back to the apartment complex. For a long time, they didn't say anything to each other. They crossed Archer Road, watching carefully for traffic, then over the lot toward Hilary's apartment building.

When they got to the sidewalk, Hilary turned to Audrey. "Did you see the dragon? The skeleton?"

"No."

"I did."

"Oh. That sounds awful."

"It was."

"Tell me about it."

"Tomorrow, okay? I just can't talk about it now."

Audrey nodded and smiled gently. "Sure. I understand. Tomorrow will be fine. See you at school."

"Okay. 'Bye."

Audrey waved and walked off across the parking lot.

Inside the front door of the building, Hilary stopped and looked at Frank's door.

Maybe I'll tell him what happened. Maybe we can be friends, too, now that all this is over.

Hilary looked up the stairs then looked down at the floor where her mother had landed. It made her shiver. "I'm so sorry, Mom!" she whispered.

Then and there Hilary decided she would do all she could to help her mother and her family from now on. No more lying. No more sneaking. No more being a brat.

"I'm going to start over with Mom, Dad, and Douglas," she said to herself as she began climbing the steps. "They're my best friends, after all. They've always been my very best friends. I'll even tell Doreen how sorry I am."

Then, from above, she could hear an apartment door open, and a familiar voice call down. "Hilary!" It was Douglas. "Is that you?"

"Yes!"

"I just got home from the hospital, and Mom's doing much better! They say she'll probably be able to come home tomorrow! Isn't that great?"

Hilary broke into a run, taking the steps two at a time. "Oh, yes! That's wonderful!" she shouted.

And it was then she realized that Illinois would be a good place to live, after all.

About the Author

Elizabeth Massie is a Bram Stoker award-winning and Scribe Award-winning author of novels and short fiction for middle grade readers, teens, and adults. Her favorite genres are historical fiction and horror fiction (which she often calls "skeery stories!") She also writes nonfiction and fiction for nationwide educational programs. A former 7th grade science teacher with 19 years in the classroom, she now spends her time writing, presenting creative writing workshops, and drawing ghosts, monsters, and other creatures—all part of her Skeeryvilletown cast of cartoon characters. She lives in the Shenandoah Valley of Virginia with her creative and wonderfully wacky counterpart, illustrator Cortney Skinner.

www.ingramcontent.com/pod-product-compliance
Lightning Source LLC
Chambersburg PA
CBHW061547250926
52052CB00010B/3099
9781941408636